Flirting with Disaster

When Love & Nature Collide

A Novel by

Janet S. Kleinman

Published by
Brighton Publishing LLC
501 W. Ray Road
Suite 4
Chandler, AZ 85225

Flirting with Disaster
When Love & Nature Collide

A Novel

by

Janet S. Kleinman

Published by
Brighton Publishing LLC
501 W. Ray Road
Suite 4
Chandler, AZ 85225
www.BrightonPublishing.com

ISBN: 13: 978-1-936587-80-3
ISBN: 10: 1-936-58780-7

Printed in the United States of America

First Edition

Cover Design By: Tom Rodriguez

❧ Foreword ❧

M any thanks to Kathie McGuire, my editor and publisher, who had faith in me and my story.

I also give thanks to the members of the Writer's Group at the Delray Beach Public Library who sat through chapter-by-chapter readings of this novel.

Thanks also to Rose Silma and Venante and Raoul Charles. These Haitian/Americans made certain my use of Haitian words and expressions were linguistically and idiomatically correct. They have become valued friends.

And to my family who encouraged me to take the risk and get *Flirting with Disaster* published and read by all of you.

❧ *Prologue* ❧

*F*orty years after our first kiss, he called.

It was a quiet, rainy Sunday evening in South Florida. *Casablanca* was on the television, and although I was in another room I could hear Ilsa ask Sam, "Play it once, Sam, for old times'sake. Play it, Sam. Play *As Time Goes By*."

It brought back memories, but I had no time to watch. I was sitting at the computer, writing the greatest story ever told (excuse me, *New Testament*) when the phone rang. I scanned the ID. The number had a "228" area code. Where had I seen it before? I closed my eyes and focused. An image of the glitzy ads the Palace Casino Resort in Biloxi, Mississippi, was running in my local newspaper appeared. 228 was the area code for hotel reservations. Since Hurricane Katrina, the Gulf Coast casinos were offering tempting vacation packages to lure tourists and gamblers back.

The name next to the number read *MGREEN*. Coincidentally, that was the first initial and the surname of my first boyfriend. But what was Mickey doing in Mississippi? And how did he find me?

The last time I heard from him, he'd enlisted in the Navy after an unsuccessful year at Mohawk University in upstate New York. Mickey had been a handsome jock—the hero and captain of the soccer team—at a high school where, at the time, the soccer team members reigned as kings. That was because it was the only team that had ever won a citywide championship for our school.

I'd been a nerdy, aloof sophomore with serious academic inclinations and a well-developed body at a young age. But when that olive-skinned athlete, a senior with dark brown eyes and a broad smile, looked my way and winked, I couldn't resist. Saturday after Saturday, he scored the winning goal and was carried across the field, his hair blowing in the wind, on the shoulders of his teammates while the crowd cheered. And he had chosen to date me.

That was in the 1960s, when both of us had raging hormones threatening to get out of control. An invisible stop sign engraved on our bodies and souls by ever-vigilant mothers put an end to any of the ultimate carnal pleasures before they began. But this didn't stop us from holding hands in the park, smooching in the back row of the local theatre—forbidden soul kisses—some petting, and fabulous imagination.

I was being ridiculous. There must be thousands of MGreens across the country and hundreds in Mississippi.

So I picked up the phone, expecting a glib sales pitch for a weekend at a casino in Biloxi. Perhaps they were offering three nights for the price of two. Or free airfare.

"Hello, is this Gloria Simon?"

"Yes."

"You've still got that sexy voice, forty years later."

"Who is this?"

"Mickey Green, remember me?"

I detected a tiny, familiar lisp. It was still there.

"Mickey Green, Mickey Green, how could I forget? How are you?"

"Good now. Had some health issues, but I'm in remission now."

"I'm glad. What are you doing in Mississippi?"

"Biloxi, to be exact. I made a ton of money in the cleaning business in Atlanta, but hated it. I'm retired and like to gamble, so living in a suite at the Palace Casino Hotel suits me fine. It's more fun."

"I heard you married after your discharge from the Navy, and that's where the trail ended."

"I'm separated, with two daughters; one's divorced, the other's mad at me. Luckily, I have a beautiful granddaughter. I went back to college after the Navy and, believe it or not, this jock became an engineer."

"You were never dumb."

"Thanks."

The conversation went on. I told him about my two children and four grandchildren, about my life up north, our move to Florida, publishing a few articles that came with bylines. He remembered me playing gin rummy with his father in their Brooklyn apartment. And I thought I had a good memory! I didn't tell him my late husband, a physician, had had Alzheimer's. In the past few years, life had grown lonelier and lonelier, even before he died.

"Can you fly to Biloxi? I'd love to meet you again," he said. "I'll pay for the ticket."

"Maybe for a night or two, but I can buy my own ticket—that is, if you teach me how to gamble. I've always wanted to play blackjack."

"Sure, why not? I'll even treat you to the first hundred dollars' worth of chips."

"Why would you want me to come? Maybe I've grown old and ugly."

"Frankly, someone we both know told me you've grown older, but look pretty good. That's how I got your phone number."

"I'd love to know who it was."

"It doesn't matter. Let's just say she's a sharp-looking redhead who lives in Palm Beach County, and that I'd like to see you for old time's sake. Those were the best years of our lives."

They had been good years, although I wasn't sure they were the best. I needed desperately to get away—to distance myself from my own problems and repressed guilt—yet I wanted to know more about my old boyfriend before I made such a radical decision. But how do you begin to ask personal questions?

"Mickey, did you ever play soccer again after high school?"

"A little when I dropped out of college. I got $25 per game playing for the New York Soccer League. It was $25 more than I had in my pocket at that time."

"So much has happened to us both."

"So, will you come to Biloxi?"

"I'm curious, and I admit I'm tempted. Let's stay in touch for a while first."

And that's how the relationship began.

❧ Chapter One ❧

I t was not quite daybreak when thunder rattled the windows. Torrents of rain fell the morning after Mickey called me. There'd be no tennis game today, so I shut off the radio alarm and crawled back into bed. I couldn't sleep. I kept thinking of those coming-of-age days, the parties after the Saturday high school home games, Plum Beach in his father's big Buick, watching the moon's reflection on the murky waters, and the thrill of being caressed by a handsome, young man.

When day broke, I bolted out of bed to block out this mature woman's insane feelings of adolescence. I'd been in love several times before I married, and hadn't thought about old boyfriends in years. I was beginning to enjoy my newfound freedom as a widow, but hadn't grown accustomed to being alone.

There were no more medicine bottles all over the house. The medical equipment company picked up the oxygen tanks weeks ago, and the sheets and pillowcases on the other side of the bed stayed clean. There was no more messy underwear to wash. After five years of caring for my once-vital and adoring husband, life had been banished from the house, but so had love.

It was too early to vacuum and wake my downstairs neighbor, so I turned on my PC. There was the usual pile of e-mail sent automatically over the weekend by insurance companies and automobile dealers, magazines soliciting subscribers, and mail-order catalogues selling sexy underwear or gimmicky kitchen gadgets. Most were destined for deletion without being read. What

I really needed was a warm message from a friend. One e-mail address had possibilities, but I couldn't tell who the sender was. I hadn't had my caffeine fix and my brain was still sluggish.

It read:

From: Papmick@hmail.net
To: Globaby@eol.com

Dear Gloria:

It was great talking to you and reminiscing about our "coming of age" together. You were younger, more innocent, yet smarter than me then. But I went off to the Navy and learned a lot—different things than you learned a few years later at college and fraternity parties, I bet. Somewhere I'm sure we caught up to each other. Girls, I've found out, mature earlier. Anyway, I'd like to know more about you. I've got time. Do you?

I know we're older now, so I'm sure we've both had lots of experiences—some good, some not so good; some happy, others sad. We should have a lot to share. I don't always remember what happened yesterday, but I'll never forget those wonderful, young years. I can still picture the way you looked and walked and attracted lots of boys. But I was your king of the hill, at least for a little while. What do you say? Will you write?

Lots of Love,

Mickey

How silly, I thought, *to start corresponding with someone I hadn't seen in forty years!* But then, it might be fun.

I heard the *Sun Post* hit the front door as the paperboy went by. It was my signal to close the computer and brew some coffee. As the smell of a Haitian blend pervaded the apartment, I went to the bathroom, took the pins out of my hair, ran a comb through it, and proceeded to open the front door. You never knew who else might be taking in their newspaper this early.

With a mug of coffee in one hand and a pen in the other, I turned my attention to my brain fitness exercises. Each morning while I ate my breakfast and drank my coffee, I did the crossword puzzle. Today's started off easy until I got to eighteen-across: "A drugged drink." To my surprise, I got it—Mickey Finn! I never saw that expression before in the daily crossword, and I've been doing them for years.

Taking my "Best Grandma" coffee mug to my desk, I turned to my PC, opened my e-mail, and hit compose.

> *From: Globaby@eol.com*
> *To: Papmick@hmail.net*

> *A little bit of trivia I thought you'd appreciate—you made it into this morning's crossword puzzle in the local paper. The definition of 18-across was "drugged drink." And I finally got it…Mickey Finn. Had to tell you.*

> *I never saw them ask for a word that means "great" in Christian worship. The answer would be Gloria. Don't even know if you like word games. I don't remember you being a book lover, either.*

> *Regards,*

> *Gloria*

The next weeks were busy ones. I spent hours in the gym, firming up my abdomen, thighs, and upper arms at a club that guaranteed a young woman's body to every older woman who completed the program. My personal trainer was relentless. I dragged myself home after each session, applied Bio-Freeze to my aching muscles, and fell asleep. I was determined to get into a size-ten dress again. And the eights? I'd better pack them up and donate them to Dress for Success, an organization that helps needy young women get jobs.

I delayed joining the singles club until I was slimmer. Most men liked their women thin, but some, I noticed, preferred them zaftig.

Threatening skies and sun showers sent me indoors on many afternoons. It was the season for doing the dozens of things I'd postponed month after month. I replaced the boxes of photographs I'd brought with me from New York. Some of my favorite albums were crumbling from age and humidity, despite the constant buzz of the air conditioner. I wanted my children to have these as part of their legacy. Carefully, I separated the baby pictures by sex, labeled new albums, and got to work. Then I mixed up the who's who of my son and daughter, grew frustrated, and left them spread out all over the dining room table.

I gravitated to the computer to play a game of solitaire, but first checked my e-mail. And there it was: the familiar "You've got mail!" It was from him.

From: Papmick@hmail.net
To: Globaby@eol.com

Dear Gloria:

I didn't intend writing to you this quickly, but after I got off the telephone, I felt nostalgic. There's lots I want to know; so much I want to tell you.

I heard there was an all-inclusive Wagner High School reunion in Boca. Did you go? Was anyone there that we both know? Was Lolly Warner there? I want to get in touch with her. Stan Josephson was my cousin. Did you know that? They were so hot for each other— even after high school—but her mother didn't approve of him. They kept in touch for years after they were both married, although his marriage didn't last too long. He died recently. I wonder if she knows. Do you have her e-mail address or phone number? I'd appreciate you sending it to me.

Right now I wish it would rain. I know you've got so much of it in Florida you could sell it to us, except there's no pipeline connecting Mississippi and Florida. Too bad, we could solve our drought, and Florida could improve its economy. So instead of taking my daily walk, I went to the casino for breakfast and won $500 playing blackjack.

This former jock has bad legs—those old soccer injuries have returned to haunt me and won't even let me work out in the gym. I'm turning into a high roller at the crap table instead, thanks to those days in the Navy when we played in the alleys of Singapore.

How are you spending your day?

P.S. Attached is a survey. Will you fill it out so I see how your likes and dislikes have changed since we were young and foolish? Of course, some of your answers will help me imagine what you look like now.

Lots of Love,

Mickey

I must admit, I was glad to have my solitaire game interrupted. You never win anyway. I reread Mickey's message and the survey, then went into compose mode.

Dear Mickey:

You saved me from a boring afternoon. I'd just mixed up the baby pictures of my children, abandoned them on the dining room table, and fled to the computer to find you there via e-mail. Reminded me of that old song that ended with "coming in on a wing and a prayer." Must be ESP.

Sorry to hear about Stan. I knew him too, and was aware that he and Lolly continued their relationship, as friends, throughout the years. She told me he served twenty years in the Navy and sent her picture postcards from exotic places all over the world. He was her first boyfriend, too. That's a special place in a girl's life. She probably doesn't know Stan died, or she would have shared the news with me.

E-mails are not her thing, but phoning her should be all right. Her number is 555-683-2109. She and her husband Mel live in the town next to Boca. Stan probably told you she had five daughters. We were classmates at college, too, so our friendship—with some interruptions—has lasted a long time. She's vulnerable now, so tread carefully. Lung cancer is spreading throughout her body, so she spends most of her time on oxygen, watching movies at home. An unexpected phone call from an old friend might be welcome because she's afraid of visitors bringing germs into the house. Her immune system is especially weak. Let me know how it all works out.

Mickey, I don't like surveys, so if you want to know if my hair is gray, just ask me. I'd like to know how you look, too. I remember an olive-skinned, muscular guy with jet-black hair—kind of Native American or Latino looking—and a big smile. There must be a recent photo of me in "My Pictures." It's only a few months since my granddaughter's Bat Mitzvah, and we took a lot. If there's a good shot, I'll forward it to you. Will you reciprocate?

Fondly,

Glo

Then I pressed send. I knew our correspondence would continue. I'd included too many *tell me* clues in my messages.

6

A day later, Lolly called me. She was not her usual doom and gloom self, but seemed upbeat for a change. The call from Mickey had been a pleasant surprise for her. They reminisced about Stan, double dates I didn't remember, and yearnings that had never materialized. She and Mickey talked for over an hour, she said, about the old crowd—so many of whom were now retired and lived in Florida's Palm Beach County.

In the 1970s, there was a mass exodus of our married classmates from Brooklyn to Long Island. Everybody was working or having babies. Some were successful, others were failures, and a few have died, including Red Perry, the captain of the basketball team who introduced Mickey and me so many years ago. Lolly seemed to know them all.

Then came the shocker. She and Mickey had spent a long time talking about her cancer—and his. His was a recurring liposarcoma I didn't quite understand. Mickey hadn't told me much about his health, just his deteriorating knees. He was very macho as a young athlete, and probably still is. Even women past their prime want to be impressed. I hadn't told him about the heart bypass that saved my life eight years ago. According to my doctor, I'm cured. Is he?

Monday night was TV comedy night for me. I loved *Two and a Half Men,* and reruns of *M*A*S*H* and *Becker.* Sometimes, during the commercials, I gravitated toward my computer. Tonight the invisible genie in the machine sang out, "You've got mail."

I felt a rush of excitement, then disappointment. The message wasn't from Mickey; it was just an ad for a dating service promising complete satisfaction. But just before I closed down, a new message surfaced in my inbox.

From: Papmick@hmail.net
To: Globaby@eol.com

Hi Glo:

I used to call you that instead of the formal Gloria. Did you receive a newsletter, the "US Annual Soccer Guide and Record"? I think it was for the '58–'59 season. In it, there's a picture of the New York Sport Club, that year's state soccer champions. I'm the one crouching down in the front row on the left—one of only two Americans on the team. I think I told you that I got $25 for playing in the final game of the season. It was no way to make a living, and I was going to be drafted anyway, so I joined the Navy. They trained me to be a weatherman, and I realized I had a brain as well as a strong pair of legs. It was time to grow up. Thanks to the G.I. Bill, this jock who you think didn't read very much decided to go back to school. I enrolled for an engineering degree at Mohawk University in Utica. Not MIT, but good enough. Coincidently, Ike Pappas—we used to call him The Greek—was studying there, too. We were known as the downstate duo, and we played winning ice hockey together just the way we played soccer at high school.

Physics and calculus were tough, but I managed to pass. I always liked to tinker with my hands and put things together, just like my dad. By the way, he always wanted to know what happened to the pretty girl I brought home one day who beat him in gin rummy. Remember?

What did you wind up doing after college?

Lots of Love,

Mickey

I replied instantly.

Dear Mickey:

Most of my girlfriends—the ones you knew, including Lolly—married the day after our college graduation and went off to army bases with their postwar-draftee husbands to what were then remote places—like Louisiana or Alabama. A year later, they were mothers.

I didn't want to marry, or perhaps there were lots of boyfriends, but none I wanted to spend my life with. I wanted to go to law school, but papa vetoed that as unnecessary for a girl, and my mother wasn't inclined to persuade him otherwise. I didn't want to teach school either, so I got a job as a secretary to the president of an advertising/public relations agency. Soon I was writing press releases and promotional materials for Fortune 500 corporations. The guys and gals who worked with me came from different backgrounds; some came from other states and countries. It wasn't long before I had a secretary of my own.

As a team, a few of us manned convention booths for our company in places I'd only read about. I loved seeing other parts of the USA...Texas, Missouri, Louisiana, the cities of New Orleans, St. Louis, and Dallas. Occasionally I'd take the Amtrak to Philadelphia for the day while working on a special project for a big drug firm. I loved the freedom of being unsupervised while working with a colleague from another company. When our writing and editing of the brochure, called "The Waiting Room," was finished, he'd take me to see the Liberty Bell and Independence Hall and we'd have dinner on cobblestoned Society Hill before I took the train back to New York. I was twenty-two, and it was wonderful. My boss, for his own puritanical reasons, kept a paternal eye on me and interfered if any of the married execs or visiting reps seemed to be getting too friendly.

Like most unmarried girls, I lived at home, and saved enough money for a trip to Europe. Mama (you remember that pretty, plump woman who was always offering you her homemade cookies when we dated) howled and cried, "Nice girls don't go to Europe alone." So I settled for an auto trip to New England and Nantucket with a female friend who'd bought herself a second-hand Chevy. All I remember about that trip was the wonderful feeling of independence and a wild evening at a bar outside the New London Naval Base with blond, blue-eyed officers who were mesmerized by two New York girls traveling solo.

Two years later, I met my husband-to-be at a friend's party. We fell in love and married six months later. Coincidently, he grew up ten blocks away from where I lived, and went to the same high school as you and me, but several years earlier. He may have known your brother; he didn't know mine. He was a doctor in the process of opening up a practice in Riverdale, a northern outpost of New York City. We started to build our future.

Fill me in about that part of your life.

Fondly,

Glo

The next day, there was another message from Mickey:

Dear Glo:

Thanks so much for making it possible for me to reach Lolly. We had a great conversation...We just went back in time and laughed at all the things we remembered about those good old days.

He told me all about Lolly's lung cancer. Mickey was genuinely upset. I'd been living with her diagnosis for several months now, and made peace with the road her illness would ultimately travel. Then he explained that a liposarcoma is a cancer that keeps coming back, and he'd had several operations at MD Anderson in Houston. His last check-up had occurred only three weeks ago, and he was still waiting for the doctor's report. Hopefully the cancer was self-contained. His e-mail continued:

Lolly tells me you've sold some articles to magazines, profiles of pretty hot movers and shakers. I'd like to read them. Will the local library have copies? Send me the names of the mags and the dates of the issues. She couldn't remember.

I like to write, too, but not your kind of writing. I'm the Biloxi's Billboard*'s regular pain in the butt, always sending letters to the editor about what's wrong with Biloxi, and now, with the presidential elections coming, views on the candidates. You still have to be a little careful around here, because the word "nigger" hasn't gone out of fashion completely, even if the one who says it thinks he might vote for Obama.*

There's a brand new Canon Sure Shot in my bottom drawer. My girls gave it to me last Father's Day, and I haven't used it yet. I'll take it with me to my breakfast club and ask one of the guys to shoot a few pics of me in different poses. I'm not any heavier, although I was a few years ago. And that jet-black hair you remember is white—all of it—but there's no bald spot. I won't be able to leave the pictures on the PC. There are reasons. I'll check them out at the local drugstore, develop the good ones, and send them to you via snail mail. By the way, I just realized I don't have your address. That would help.

Waiting for you to write again.

Lots of Love,

Mickey

❧ *Chapter Two* ❧

Every time I checked my inbox, there was a new message from Mickey with an attachment. The "Maxine" cartoons, about a spirited old lady adjusting to the younger generation and their wireless world, were funny. So were some of the jokes, but most had been recycled and repeated dozens of times since early television variety shows.

I thanked Mickey for the Maxine cartoons. I think she was the first feminist in the twentieth century; she sure looked old enough. Then I deleted everything else. *It's over,* I thought. We have nothing more to say to each other. But then something happened, and I had to write to him.

From: Globaby@eol.com
To: Papmick@hmail.net

Dear Mickey:

Sorry to have to break the news, but Lolly died this morning. She was in hospice the last few days. Her lung cancer had spread everywhere. I'm so sorry that her daughters wouldn't let anyone see her for the last few weeks, but everyone has their own feelings about death and dying. The funeral is in New York and I have no idea how long her husband will be staying up north with his daughters, certainly for the mourning period. I'd send condolences to the house in Florida. Mel, her husband, will get the mail eventually.

13

I'm not too big on attachments, unless they're exceptionally funny, but I would like to know more about you personally.

Fondly,

Gloria

The rainy season lingered on. Playing bridge on the computer and attempting to finish my neglected photo albums—I called them "From Infancy to First Birthdays"—wasn't enough to fill the long days. I took a sculpture class and enjoyed the sensation of wet clay in my hands and on my fingers. I was determined to create a Grecian head. I closed my eyes and envisioned my first love as an athletic hero entering a stadium. It didn't work. I could visualize the form, but couldn't duplicate it in clay.

Instead I copied a piece of modern sculpture, a stringed figure by Henry Moore that I'd seen in a museum at the University of Wisconsin last summer. My rendition was a disaster. The strings of wire wouldn't hold up the right side of the figure; the left side fell apart. I rolled the clay into a ball, covered it with damp newspaper, and stored it away for another day. So it was back to solitaire or e-mail, anything to occupy the time.

I logged on, and there was the welcome announcement: "You've got mail."

From: Papmick@hmail.net
To: Globaby@eol.com

Dear Glo:

Found your address in the AOL directory. A photo is on the way to you. It's a little blurred and not as pretty as yours, but you'll see that I'm not bald or fat.

I haven't written lately because I'm depressed. I got the report from the Houston hospital. The liposarcoma is back, but luckily most of the cells are dead. It'll probably take a few years before they grow again, but they can operate if my health and heart remain good.

I'm depressed about other things, too. My only granddaughter, who's a college sophomore, is screwing around with a boy from Haiti. I know I'm supposed to be broadminded about race and origins, but that's easier when it is someone else's grandkid. When it's your own, I'd prefer she choose a Caucasian like myself. Also, he's not exactly an upstanding guy; he's been arrested twice for breaking and entering automobiles, but she tells me he's reformed. He works for an Atlanta construction company that's remodeling the dorms at her school and he attends classes at night, so he's always around.

Do I stop paying her tuition? I'm afraid if I do that, she might elope with him. My oldest daughter, her mother, ran off to the Bahamas with a lover, leaving a beautiful twelve-year-old child—and her husband— behind. I haven't talked with her since. Judith and I helped Mitch, her ex, raise Melissa. In fact she lived with us during the last two years of high school after her father remarried.

My younger daughter is a successful attorney, but she and her husband don't want children.

The only place we forget about our family problems is at the casino. If we drive up to Tunica, like we did during last year's hurricane, we have nine casinos to choose from, and we can play poker or blackjack all day and night.

Lots of Hugs & Kisses,

Mickey

I reread the e-mail and thought, *Who the hell are we?*

I copied the soccer bulletin Mickey sent me, intending to drive to the post office and mail it to my grandsons in California. They're both stars on Oakland's Junior Soccer League. My son Keith coaches the older boys' team; his wife Rachel, who played women's soccer at college, coaches the younger one's team.

To my delight, they all invited themselves to Florida for the Thanksgiving holidays. My daughter and her family, who live in North Carolina, were also coming. We were finally going to have a family reunion. *Too bad Ted is gone*, I thought. It would have made him so happy.

There was one problem: where would we all sleep? The boys offered to bring their sleeping bags; they're habitual campers. And the rest of us—well, for the sake of togetherness, we'd manage.

I should have been very happy about this reunion, but I was kind of blue. It was a year since my son, an MBA from Harvard, lost his job. It had not been the time to argue with his supervisor, but I didn't say anything. He couldn't seem to find his niche in the California business world. He's luckier than other young fathers in this economy; his wife is a successful trial lawyer.

After reading the morning paper, however, I enclosed a postscript for him with the sports section; Joey Metro, a pitcher, had been asked to report for spring training by the Florida Marlins after being sent back to the minors after a dismal season. He was quoted as saying, "I've had success before; I will have success again."

Do we ever stop worrying about our adult children?

Watching the Florida economy sink deeper into recession upset me. My personal life was tied to the ups and downs of the financial markets, and they didn't appear promising. Not even the political name-calling and exaggerated flag-waving of the Republican, Democratic, and Tea Party candidates could overshadow the countless empty shops dotting malls all over the county.

I needed to share my feelings with someone, but girlfriends are such gossips. I decided to write to Mickey once more. He'd shared some personal things about his family with me—albeit not enough—and didn't travel in the same social circles, so it would remain confidential.

> *From: Globaby@eol.com*
> *To: Papmick@hmail.net*
>
> *Dear Mickey:*
>
> *Sorry I haven't written sooner, but I'm in a good/bad mood. Good, because I just found out both my children and their families are coming to Florida for Thanksgiving. Bad, because my son, the Harvard graduate, can't keep his mouth shut. He argued with his supervisor and—I just found out—got fired a few months ago. I won't give him any advice, because he doesn't value my suggestions. Any ideas?*
>
> *Gloria*

Mickey must have been sitting at his computer in Biloxi waiting for word from me. A message came back immediately.

> *From: Papmick@hmail.net*
> *To: Globaby@eol.com*
>
> *Don't worry about your son. I was in the same situation, and my wife couldn't get me to move my ass (excuse me!) and look for a job. I didn't coach a team, but tinkered in my basement workshop and eventually designed a gadget that was used on the original moon landing. It's true. I went from the drawing board to*

hawking my gadget to the US Government Procurement Office. I was on a roll until Congress cut the funds for NASA. The locator became obsolete, its function incorporated into a more sophisticated computer. My original patent expired, and my business went belly-up. I think it was during the '80s recession.

I needed to support my family, so I borrowed some money from my brother Jack, who was the dry-cleaning czar of Broward County, and opened a store of my own in Atlanta. Eventually I had a string of them, and the bucks kept rolling in. All cash, no credit, no billing.

Boring—but so what? I built a big house in Atlanta, and after a few years hired a manager, sent the girls to expensive colleges, and took a six-week vacation to Europe. Then I started feeling sick and had lots of tests. That's when my liposarcoma was diagnosed. It was a death sentence. I sold the stores and found I could forget about my terminal cancer by gambling. I was attracted to the Gulf Coast. But I got lucky; my cancer went into remission. For how long, no one knows. I might live a long time or die tomorrow, so I built a second home in Biloxi. I call it Paradise.

I wish our girls were coming to Mississippi for the holidays, but my youngest who filed for divorce not too long ago, after being married for twenty-five years, is dating her would-be ex again. She likes him better as a boyfriend than as a husband. Women's instinct...my wife knew it was coming before we were told. Things were different when we were growing up. Divorce was not in our vocabulary. That's why I slip into "we" mode now and then.

I'm still married. I met Judith when I got out of the Navy. I was as horny as hell, so it was a quick romance. She was a pretty blonde, but somehow after two kids and a number of years the attraction diminished. We talked about divorce, but never did anything about it. Life has been comfortable if not exciting. She's not as inquisitive as you, so we watch a lot of television. As I remember, you were interested in everything—music, art, theatre, sports. You would have taken me kicking and screaming into a world we would have enjoyed together. But she has taken good care of me, especially when I've been ill, and I appreciate her for that.

She likes to gamble, too. Do you? And does it really matter that I'm still married? Please don't stop writing.

Lots of Love and Kisses,

Mickey

I didn't bother to respond. I'd found out enough about Mickey for one day. I liked men, but married ones were nothing but trouble. I'd learned that as a young woman.

There were so many couples in this condo complex who lived together but wouldn't marry, and I don't mean young ones. I've heard all kinds of excuses; "The children wouldn't like it." "We'd only get one Social Security check." "What'd happen if I gave up my apartment, moved into his, and he died? His heirs would likely ask me to move out."

I realized it was nearly one p.m. I banished my troubling thoughts, dressed quickly, and had a light lunch. My bridge game started in half an hour, and arriving late was a no-no with the other players.

I decided to mail the soccer programs to my grandsons the next day.

❧ Chapter Three ❧

I didn't hear from Mickey for several weeks, and tried to forget his last e-mail. But a line stuck with me—"does it really matter that I'm still married?"

I flew to New York City for a two-week vacation and had a great time. I'd left a message on my computer: "Please send no messages between July 25 and August 10. I will be away. Resume sending on August 11."

I soaked in the culture of the city, savoring its museums, attending the theatre and concerts, and visiting friends. I talked with strangers I met on buses and at art exhibits. It was lonely at night when I came back to the apartment I'd rented in my old neighborhood. Only a cold, flat screen TV kept me company in the room with the queen-sized bed.

South Florida was being flooded by Haitian immigrants, some legal, others not. They braved rough seas and dishonest ship captains to make the journey. Their country was the poorest in the Western Hemisphere. These ragged newcomers needed to escape the poverty that kept their children hungry, and the government corruption that provided inferior hospitals, understaffed schools, and few jobs for the poor.

Since I'd been a teacher in another place, at another time, I wanted to do something important not only for the children, but also for their mothers and fathers. I called the county literacy agency and offered to teach Haitian immigrants to read. They were glad to have me. The local libraries supplied small, private rooms where we worked with our students. Some of my students grasped the unfamiliar sounds of English, and it was rewarding to see their progress; others exerted little effort to augment our lessons by studying, and failed.

The students came and went; they stopped coming if they got a job, or decided to return to Haiti. A few were serious, especially a refined older man with gray running through his curly black hair. He'd been a banker in Haiti until a revolutionary government confiscated most of his assets and took possession of the family bank. Then he'd escaped imprisonment by booking passage on a decrepit fishing boat that, luckily, didn't sink. His name was Henri Betencourt.

As the lesson progressed, he'd try to caress my hands when I pointed to passages in the workbooks the agency provided, and he kept moving his chair closer to mine.

I'd look at his handsome black face and say, "Henri, this is a reading lesson; no touching, no feeling."

He'd laugh.

During one of the lessons, I closed the rather elementary workbook and took a local newspaper out of my tote bag.

"Here," I said, handing him the paper. "Find something you'd like to read. Use the headlines to guide you."

On the third page was an article about two young Haitian men who had reached shore in an inflated dinghy before being apprehended by the police. Would they be allowed to stay? He smiled at me, a big, toothy grin, and continued to read.

The library's closing time approached.

"That's enough for today, Henri."

"Yes, Miss Simon. I'll see you next week." He folded the newspaper and handed it back to me.

"Keep it, Henri. Finish the story when you get home."

I left before my student. A block from the library, I noticed a green Chevy that seemed to be following me. Five minutes later, when I was about to enter the condo gates, the same car was still there. The gatekeeper let me in; the Chevy made a U-turn before reaching the inner gate, left the entrance, and returned to the road.

Once upstairs, I double-locked my door, took a deep breath, and went to the computer.

From: Globaby@eol.com
To: Papmick@hmail.net

Too bad you're in Biloxi. Married or not I'd ask for your protection.

A six-foot Haitian student followed me home. He seemed to get too personal during our study session. I'm scared. Should I call the police or the Palm Beach Literacy Agency or the FBI? For all I know, Henri Betencourt is an illegal alien. I don't want to get him into trouble.

Fondly,

Gloria

I pushed send and waited. A half hour later, there was a message from Mississippi.

From: Papmick@hmail.net
To: Globaby@eol.com

Lock your door! Keep it locked whenever you're at home.

I've wanted to make up with my brother Jack for a long time. He's in Broward County. I'd fly over if I could stay with you. No shenanigans. You stay in your bedroom,

I'll sleep on the couch. Don't worry, I'll take care of you. By the way, I have a license to carry a gun.

Write soon.

Hugs & Kisses,

Mickey

Mickey's reference to a gun made me shiver despite the Florida heat.

If he came here and encountered Henri, what would happen? I didn't think my student was the militant type. Although he wasn't young, there was a sexual animalism about him...the way he walked, the way he looked at me as if imagining what was underneath my sundress. I guessed that he'd left a woman behind in Haiti and was lonely for female companionship, but that was just conjecture. I knew he loved his country.

I watched the maintenance crew at my condo. I had no idea about how they earned a living in Haiti, but here they nursed our gardens with a passion that made them flower with exotic blooms throughout the seasons. The Creole language flowed from their lips and seemed to make the women who cleaned the buildings smile. Even the fat ones wore tight tops; the men were always patting their behinds. It seemed that touching was an integral part of their culture.

Maybe Mickey was being overaggressive. It seemed that he needed to do something heroic not only to impress me, but also to bolster his own machismo. I refrained from issuing a serious invitation for Mickey to come save me from Henri.

I was scheduled to see Henri again on Thursday. Somehow I wasn't afraid, but I decided to leave the study room door slightly ajar.

As I considered all this, the doorbell rang.

"Who is it?"

"Delivery."

"Of what?"

"Flowers."

I peeked out the kitchen window. There was a teenager in a thin windbreaker holding a large bouquet of native Floridian flowers—asters, tuberoses, and yellow daisies.

I took a dollar from my wallet, and then hid my tote bag in the washing machine. Leaving the chain on, I opened the door. The boy couldn't squeeze the bouquet through the opening so, with a trembling hand, I unhooked the chain, took the flowers, pushed the tip into his small clenched fist, and slammed the door shut, locking it immediately.

There was no card with the flowers. I looked over the catwalk rail and watched the boy get into the passenger side of a green Chevy. Someone drove him away.

From: Papmick@hmail.net
To: Globaby@eol.com

Hon:

Are you all right? I contacted my brother Jack. He'd like to let bygones be bygones. Anxious to keep you safe. When shall I come?

A little love,

Mickey

I wasn't going to tell him about the flowers. It was easier to ignore his e-mail.

Thursday came. At four-thirty p.m., I was at the library waiting for Henri. He arrived minutes after me, impeccably dressed in a gray pin-striped suit and carrying a faux leather briefcase.

"Hi, Ms. Simon. I'm here and ready to study."

"Good. Did you read the newspaper article we started the other day?

"I thought I knew one of the young men—only eighteen. He looked like a friend's son. All the young men try to leave Haiti, and some of the older ones, too. There is no future in my homeland. So I hurried over to the Boynton Beach Police Station. The officer let me speak with the boy. By the time the Haitian Immigrant Friends Society representative arrived, Pierre and I were friends. I swore I'd do everything I could to allow him to stay in the United States. He doesn't want to go back."

I kept looking at the neatly pressed suit. Had he dressed up for our reading class?

"Anyway," he continued, "the society is overloaded with cases, and after watching me with Pierre, they asked if I'd like a job as a *cresis* counselor for Haitians in trouble. Did I pronounce that right?"

"The first syllable has a long i, and the word is pronounced crisis."

"I told them I was studying English, especially the written word. It's important so I can help the detainees with their paperwork and writing home to their families. Some of the boys from the remote villages are illiterate. My sincerity pleased the man from the agency.

"As of today I am employed as a cresis...no, no...crisis counselor for Haitians in trouble. Do I look the part? I must make my charges feel confident. I bought this suit this morning at a fancy consignment shop in West Palm. Does it fit all right?"

With Henri's build, any suit would look good, but all I said was, "It fits perfectly."

Without thinking, but meaning it, I hugged him. I was so proud of Henri. Then we continued with our lesson. I forgot to leave the door ajar. I forgot to ask him if he liked gardening.

We left the library at the same time. As we neared my red Toyota, we stopped. "Did you like your flowers, Ms. Simon? I picked them myself."

"It isn't my birthday. Why did you send them?"

"You are a very patient teacher, and I'm grateful. I'm too old to bring you an apple. That is an American custom, isn't it?"

"Yes, but usually for children."

"I'm living in my brother's house in Lake Worth. He has a nice garden, like the one our family had in Haiti. His wife is a botanist and raises wildflowers. When I was still a successful banker in Haiti, I sent my brother to medical school in the Dominican Republic. He's never forgotten that. Now I'm employed again—as a crisis counselor. I have you to thank for making my English better."

Henri left me at my car and headed toward his own, a green Chevy.

I was tired and confused. Here I was thinking about an ex-boyfriend I hadn't seen in forty years, while enjoying the attentions of an illegal Haitian immigrant who claimed to have been a prosperous banker in Port-au-Prince before the old government was overthrown.

I gravitated to the computer, not exactly sure why. I turned it on, and there it was.

From: Papmick@hmail.net
To: Globaby@eol.com

Dear Gloria:

Sorry to disappoint you. I won't be able to fly to Florida because we've got a family problem in Atlanta. My only granddaughter is planning to elope with a creep she met at college. He isn't a Phi Beta Kappa or even a C student—just a maintenance man who's trying to invent a robotic sweeper. And he's black. I'm not that broad-minded when it concerns my own granddaughter; neither is her grandmother.

We're flying to Atlanta tonight to break it up, even if I have to bribe or beat him, or take her out of school, since I'm paying her tuition. He's probably nothing more than a gold-digger who wants to strike it rich. I'd like to move Melissa off campus and put her and her grandmother up in an Atlanta condo. I wouldn't trust her to commute. Her grandmother can drive her to school and keep an eye on her. If that works out, I'd fly back to Biloxi. I'm still worried about you, although I know you're smart enough to take care of yourself. Or are you? You'd be better off with a married lover than a Haitian refugee who's looking to marry a pretty American woman so he won't be deported.

Be careful.

It might not be proper for me to sleep at your house in Palm Beach County. The neighbors would never stop gossiping. Maybe you'll come to me, and I could teach you to be a high roller. The Hotel Gulfsun is very elegant, and you probably won't meet anyone you know in Biloxi. I'll foot the bill. If neither idea appeals to you, then what about meeting me in Miami? Jack and I can make up another time.

Brother or no brother, I want to see you.

Lots of Love,

Mickey

He made no mention of his gun. I was glad about that, but I wasn't happy.

From: Globaby@eol.com
To: Papmick@hmail.net

You'd better get adjusted to the fact that the world is growing browner by the minute. Have you ever met Melissa's boyfriend? Is he a nice guy? Maybe he's the next Thomas Edison. Would you object if he were Barack Obama, running for president?

Henri is the best student I've ever had. Since he's younger than me, he probably just wants to be my friend. He's educated, well-read (although much of what he reads is written in French), and highly intelligent. Every Tuesday, we discuss Maureen Dowd's column on the current political scene; on Thursdays, Thomas Friedman's column, which is more global. We argue the pros and cons of their views.

He's invited me to meet his family on Sunday. I wouldn't commit, but said I'd check my calendar. Do you think I should go?

By the way, I hope you're not taking your gun to Atlanta.

Fondly,

Gloria

I knew there was no time for Mickey to respond since he was flying to Atlanta later in the evening. I didn't really want his opinion, but I wanted him to feel it was important to me. I'd decide myself.

As I went to the hall closet to hang up my jacket, I saw that a white envelope had been slipped under the door. It was an invitation.

You are cordially invited to a cotillion
introducing our daughter Nokia
to the Haitian community
Sunday, August 30, 2008 at 8 p.m.

Columbian Court
Palm Beach, Florida
RSVP Dr. & Mrs. Pierre Betencourt
3090 Creolean Boulevard
Lantana, Florida 35610

A handwritten note had been added carefully to the bottom:

Since the party is only a few days away, please call me at 555-432-6060. I want to make sure that my sister-in-law seats you next to me for the dinner part of the gala. Do you dance?

Impatiently waiting for your reply,

Henri

I was impressed. This was more than an introduction to his family, more than a coming out party. I was being introduced to a community. What was Henri thinking?

❧ *Chapter Four* ❧

ike a grande dame, the Columbian Court is over eighty years old. It remains a beautiful hotel. I'd been there ages ago with my Uncle Eric; we'd danced into the early hours of the morning.

The structure surrounded a Spanish-style courtyard filled with exotic plants and lush palm trees. The famous chef Daniel Boulud prepared culinary masterpieces at the café and catered affairs like the party the Betencourts were throwing for their daughter, Henri's niece.

Henri would meet me there. I wore a sea-mist Holly Harper chiffon dress with an irregular hemline that resembled petals. I'd worn it to my son's wedding and, amazingly, it still fit.

I drove to Palm Beach wearing my lovely dress with an old pair of loafers I kept in the Toyota. Before I turned the car over to the parking attendant, I slipped into my favorite high-heeled, silver dancing sandals, which I'd brought along. Henri was leaning against a column to the right of the hotel entrance, watching every move I made. He was wearing a midnight blue tuxedo with satin lapels, and he looked very handsome. I smiled as I walked towards him. He held out his hands, took mine, and looked me over from the top of my head to my painted red toenails.

"Good evening, Gloria. You look lovely tonight. I'm so glad you said yes."

It was the first time he'd called me by my first name. I smiled as he mispronounced the short version of the "o."

"Thank you. You look good, too."

He escorted me to the bar in the courtyard where his brother Pierre and sister-in-law Jeanmarie were having cocktails. He introduced me and ordered two mojitos. Before we could begin to talk, guests surrounded the hosts with congratulatory messages, and they all drifted away.

"Too bad, Gloria. You'll have to meet them another time."

The bartender set down a plate of fried plantain strips before he served our drinks. We clicked glasses, and I heard myself saying, "To a lovely evening."

The decorated ballroom echoed with words of Creole, French, Spanish, and English. The men were dressed in white dinner jackets or tuxedos; the women wore low-cut dresses with side slits showing off their shapely legs. They favored floral or tropical-bird prints in brilliant shades of scarlet, yellow, and green. I realized that I was one of only a few white people there. It was a new experience for me. I'd taught and been with island people before, but not in such numbers in an enclosed space. It felt a little strange. Relax, I told myself. How would Henri feel if the numbers were reversed?

Henri was a graceful dancer, easy to follow. We went from cha-chas, meringues, and sambas to some steps that were new to me but familiar to many of the other dancers. The food was Creole, a bit too hot for my palate, but I pretended to enjoy each course. Even the filet mignon was served with rice and beans.

We skipped dessert and went outside. Henri signaled to the driver of the hotel's complimentary limo, who drove us to the nearby beach. I took off my shoes and dipped my feet into the cool ocean. It felt wonderful. Then we walked along the shore, and Henri finally took my hand.

The chauffeur had waited for us. We returned to the hotel before midnight. Henri tipped the driver, and they exchanged a few words in Creole.

The party was over. Groups of guests were leaving. I handed the valet the ticket for my car; it arrived in minutes.

"Thank you for a wonderful evening, Henri. I'll see you in class on Tuesday."

"You'll have to meet *la fanmi* another time."

He said nothing more, but leaned over and brushed his lips against my cheek.

I got into the car and, slipping off my silver sandals, put my feet back into my worn loafers and drove home.

It had indeed been a lovely evening.

I wasn't crazy about night driving, but my vision was good and I knew the roads, so I felt secure. I tried not to let my thoughts wander after such a great evening, but it was hard to keep them at bay when stopped at a red light.

Strangely, I found myself continuing to think about Mickey. He wasn't a bad guy. He was a staunch Obama supporter, and had quietly raised thousands of dollars for the candidate's campaign—in a Republican stronghold. After all, his granddaughter's welfare was more important to him than mine. I wondered if he'd taken a laptop to Atlanta with him.

It was past midnight when I parked my car and went upstairs. The first thing I did when I got inside was stretch my tired toes. I hadn't danced so much in years. Then I slipped out of my chiffon dress and left it in the middle of the living room floor. I'd hang it up in the morning. My body ached all over, but it was a happy kind of feeling.

The evening had been stimulating, and I was too charged up to consider getting into bed. I paced up and back from the bedroom to the kitchen and drank some tea. Then I went to my desk and turned on my computer.

There was only one message.

From: Papmick@hmail.net
To: Globaby@eol.com

Dear Gloria:

I'm calmer now that I've seen my granddaughter Melissa. I didn't mean to sound like a racist, but I don't like Wilson, and he brings out the worst in me. She's promised to wait until she graduates before making any long-term decisions about her boyfriend. Maybe by then the romance will have cooled off.

She's agreed to live with her grandmother, as long as she can commute to school alone. Judy, my wife, has enough old friends in Atlanta to keep herself busy.

You'll be pleased to know that I didn't take my gun with me. I've never used it—not even once—as a weatherman in the Navy, but I was a good shot and have a marksmanship medal in my drawer.

Here's the kicker, although it's probably too late. Do I think you should go to the party with your student? No. Don't give him false hope. As a teen, you didn't think I was good enough for your future. And at that time, I wasn't. And now at your age, this guy is all wrong. You live in different worlds, and there's no time to change either one of them. Can you be friends? That's another story. But how long can a man and woman remain friends without getting intimate? You tell me.

33

Love & Kisses,

Mickey

I found it hard to fall asleep that night.

For the next few days, I kept myself busy readying a PowerPoint presentation on healthcare reform for the local women's club, all the while anticipating my next English lesson with Henri—and more messages from Mickey.

Comparing these two men who had suddenly come into my life was impossible. One was younger; the other more experienced. One was healthy; the other was dealing with the ills of aging. Henri was here; I hadn't seen Mickey in forty years. One represented an unfamiliar culture; Mickey's background was what I was comfortable with, although he was married and had an addiction to gambling. Both his wife and his gambling left big holes in my comfort zone. And I could not escape the reality that one man was black, and the other white.

One day, I stopped at Barnes & Noble and bought a book titled *A Taste of Haiti.* I was surprised by how simple Haitian cooking was. Sitting in my favorite leather chair, I scanned the pages in the small volume and copied a list of ingredients Henri might buy for his own kitchen. We'd study and translate these words into English at our next lesson. I also picked up a menu from a small Haitian restaurant tucked away in the corner of one of the Military Trail malls. We could practice ordering dinner in Creole, French, or English, whatever our preference, if the first lesson was successful.

I dozed for a moment, and saw us both sitting at a corner table, holding hands. Two voluptuous Haitian women, arms bare, breasts covered in brilliant colored cotton wraparounds, stared down at us knowingly from a painting on the wall. For some reason, I felt embarrassed. The book fell out of my lap and startled me as it hit the tiled floor with a bang.

I picked up *A Taste of Haiti* and took it to my desk. There I highlighted three dishes that tempted my palate. For the appetizer, *Boulet Pomdete Ak Mori (croquettes de morue)*—salted codfish croquettes; the entree, *Poul Neg Maron Ak Kalaou (poulet avec gumbo et champignons)*—chicken, okra and mushrooms; and for dessert, *Konfiti Mango (confiture de mangue)*—mango chutney. I didn't know if Henri cooked, but I expected he would enjoy this lesson.

I suddenly realized that I had a lot of shopping to do for myself, since I'd invited guests for breakfast later in the week. Yom Kippur, the Day of Atonement, was only three days away. My guests would be hungry after not having eaten for twenty-four hours in preparation for the holiest day of the Jewish year. When the shofar (ram's horn) was blown in the synagogue at the end of the services, they would hurry home with me where we would break bread, drink wine, and devour the traditionally smoked salmon, whitefish, and herring filets, along with salads, and braided breads and bagels.

I thought for a moment of inviting Henri, but the meal would be totally alien to him. I also suspected he had no idea why we celebrated, just as I had no idea why voodoo continued to be practiced in a Catholic country. Anyway, I wasn't ready to introduce my student to any of my friends.

What was similar was that both cultures embraced hospitality, served lots of seasonal fruits and vegetables, and celebrated many holidays.

I didn't dare e-mail Mickey. I wasn't sure whether Judy had access to his laptop. I knew that in Mississippi they each had their own computer and e-mailed one another to avoid domestic arguments.

I refined my lesson for Henri, and then typed my own shopping list. The iconic "You've got mail!" appeared on my screen. I forced myself to print out both the lesson and the shopping list before I read the e-mail.

The message was from Mickey.

From: Papmick@hmail.net
To: Globaby@eol.com

Dear Gloria:

I'm still in Atlanta. No use heading back to Biloxi until Yom Kippur is over. I haven't joined the new synagogue there because I don't believe in organized religion. I know you do. Maybe I'll try it again one of these days.

I might get to Florida before you ever visit Biloxi. Judy's brother-in-law, who lives down the road from you, is in bad shape. We used to play golf together. He has lung cancer and is coughing up globs of blood every day. He can hardly breathe, and it's beginning to affect his heart. The family is considering hospice. If I stop there before going back to Biloxi, I'll figure out a way to see you. Judy will have to stay behind to keep an eye on Melissa.

Otherwise…Shana Tova to you.

Hugs & Kisses,

Mickey

P.S. Judy sometimes uses this laptop, so wait until I get back to Mississippi before writing. I'll telephone you if I get to Florida. Miss hearing from you, but when I do again, your e-mails will be all the more welcome.

I didn't appreciate the postscript on Mickey's last message. It was never a good idea to cause a feud between a husband and wife. It made more sense not to write at all.

I turned my thoughts to mundane matters. The kitchen was being remodeled next week, and the contractor had given me a ring of Formica samples for the countertops. I perused them and settled on three possibilities, but found myself wondering which one Henri would choose—the simplest, the friendliest, or the most dramatic?

What difference did it really make? Would Henri and I ever cook together?

The phone rang. It was a wrong number. I tossed the three samples into my briefcase. Maybe I'd show them to Henri on Tuesday.

Tuesday crept into my life amid the roll of thunder, flashes of lightning, and an alarming e-mail.

From: Papmick@hmail.com
To: Globaby@eol.com

Dear Glo:

I arrive at Fort Lauderdale Airport tonight at 7:30 p.m., Delta Flight 618. Keep your cell phone charged. I'll try to reach you via public phone; I left my cell in Atlanta. My brother-in-law doesn't expect me until tomorrow. It's storming here, but no flights have been cancelled yet. Keep checking with Delta. If my flight is cancelled, I'll reach you tomorrow.

Do I need to rent a hotel room? I hope not.

Hugs & Kisses

Mickey

Mickey's message and visit had come too soon. I needed to know more about him. But it was his last question—"Do I need to rent a hotel room?"—that upset me the most.

I wasn't ready. A part of me wanted him to spend the night here, but the rest of me knew it would be better if he spent it in a hotel. It was too startling to have him invade my space before we'd even had a face-to-face meeting. It had been forty years, after all. We needed to share a drink or go out on a traditional date. I'd been physically intimate with only one man since my husband died, and that had been just moderately satisfactory.

I suddenly got an urge to clean. That's a woman's thing when she wants to escape reality or decision-making. I started scrubbing corners of the apartment that hadn't seen a mop for ten years. A pair of Merry Maids was coming tomorrow, but they didn't usually find the corners anyway.

After I was sure I had the most immaculate condo in the complex, I showered and changed my clothes. I don't know why, but I felt like wearing pink, and the freshly dry-cleaned linen pants looked good on me. I then donned a matching shirt. At three-thirty, it was time to leave for my class at the library. Henri would be waiting.

He was there already, sitting at a table in front of our designated work space, intently studying his Haitian Creole–English dictionary. I tiptoed up behind him, put my hands on his shoulders, and peered into the book. Henri was on page seventy-six and had boxed in eight words and terms—starting with finance, followed by finance charge, financial aid, and ending with financing. His clean-shaven face brushed mine as he lip-synced more English words.

I moved closer to him.

My lips touched his cheek; then he pulled away. "Sorry. I thought you wouldn't mind," I whispered.

"I don't. It felt nice." Henri closed his dictionary.

"No need to do that. Why those words, Henri?"

"For the *ovai,* for the future. Someday I will deal with economics again."

"I know. But today, let's concentrate on good things to eat. Dinner, maybe? My treat."

"I couldn't let you—"

"You pay for dessert—*pouding dire* or *pen patat.*"

"Okay, rice pudding and sweet potato pie. We'll share."

"Meanwhile, it's early. Let's study."

We went into the cubicle I'd reserved. I'd prepared worksheets with lists of fruits, vegetables, staples, fowl, and cuts of beef, with columns for translation and more space for using words in sentences. I laughed at his mispronunciations; he laughed at mine. We were in no hurry to end tonight's session.

The library closed at seven o'clock. Ten minutes before they would have escorted us out, we packed up and left. I wrote down the simple directions to Café Jeba, the little Haitian restaurant I'd found; it turned out he'd been there before. Then I tossed my tote bag into the back of my Toyota and drove off with Henri following in his old green Chevy.

The restaurant stayed open until ten p.m. The dinner was delicious; the desserts even better. Henri reached across the table and had me taste a spoonful of his *pouding dire.* I reciprocated with a taste of my sweet potato pudding. We were one step closer to our lips meeting.

The rain had returned and the wind was blowing. Lightning lit up the tables; thunder shook the walls. By nine-thirty, we were the only diners left. You could hear the fronds swishing against the bark of the palms.

"More coffee, my new friends? No one should go out in this weather," the proprietor said.

Henri and I looked at each other. I nodded.

"Why not?" he said.

The cordial host brought it to us himself.

While we had our coffee, I said, "Henri, tell me about your life in Haiti. Start at the beginning."

But the rain had stopped. Even the help were leaving the restaurant.

"Another time, Gloria."

I started to take out my credit card.

"You won't need that, madam. The bill has already been paid."

Henri must have taken care of it while I'd been in the ladies' room, but it was not the time to argue about it. He walked me to my car. "*Bonswa*, my friend," he said, using Haitian Creole to say good night.

He kissed my cheek, got into his car, and drove off. So did I. As soon as I was out of the parking lot, I switched on the radio. There was a news flash. *Fort Lauderdale Airport has just reopened after a two-hour delay. No planes will be allowed to land before midnight; many flights north of Florida have been cancelled; Atlanta's airport remains closed due to flooding.*

I was relieved. Mickey wouldn't arrive tonight.

✂ *Chapter Five* ❧

Candid photos of Barack Obama and John McCain clogged every channel of my television. I wasn't in the mood for promises, the trademark of political candidates. I wanted to be optimistic about the last decades of my life; I looked forward to a world at peace and a nation climbing out of recession. The presidential candidates had their own visions for reform, but seemed to be ignoring our nation's needs.

Obama, McCain, and their respective entourages were whistle-stopping across Florida, luring voters to the polls with millions of dollars of promises. In six weeks, the employed and the unemployed, the native-born and the naturalized, would together choose the next president of the United States. A three o'clock town meeting was scheduled at the civic center, and I was planning to be there.

Politics or boyfriends, it didn't matter. I had ordinary things to do. It was the time of the month when I had to write some checks. One was to Henri Betencourt, for the sum of $28. I sent a note with it.

A deal's a deal! I was treating dinner; you were responsible for dessert. Please accept this check in the spirit in which it was written. It is approximately the cost of two entrees.

41

I loved the rice pudding. Next time you get a promotion or a job in finance or banking, you can pay for dinner and I'll pay for dessert.

Gloria

I slipped the note and check into an envelope and left it on my desk. I wasn't sure whether to mail it or give it to Henri next week.

I dressed carefully in a flared beige skirt, cropped batik jacket, and mocha patent-leather sandals. A well-dressed woman gets noticed, even at a political rally.

The civic center was only five minutes from my home. I left my house at two o'clock, knowing it would be crowded. Of course, streets were blocked off near the center, and police patrolled every entrance. I pulled into an underused mall parking lot and walked the last half-mile to join the line waiting to get inside. It gave me time to think.

I hadn't heard from Mickey. No airplane crashes had been reported. Maybe his flight had never left Atlanta because of the weather. Perhaps he would arrive today. I knew I would eventually hear from him. For now, I didn't have to make any decision about him sleeping over.

Protesters were everywhere. They carried pro-abortion or anti-abortion signs; pro-immigration or anti-immigration placards. There were slogans and more slogans. "Send More Troops to Iraq"; Finish off the Muslim Bastards"; "Bring Our Boys Home from Afghanistan." And, of course, "We Need Jobs, Not War." There were as many in Spanish as there were in English…and a few in the Creole language I was beginning to understand.

When I was finally admitted my purse was searched. I understood the fear of a possible assassination attempt, for I remembered the dreadful days following the violent, untimely deaths of John F. Kennedy, then his brother Robert. JFK was killed on my birthday. A uniformed security officer gave me a sticker for my jacket and returned my purse.

I found a single seat midway down the center aisle, and settled into a rather uncomfortable space between two obese people. I rearranged the contents of my purse and tried to relax. The meeting hadn't begun, but there was buzzing all around me. An inveterate people watcher, I looked around at the audience. Several rows in front of me, I spotted a stocky man with white hair, a lock of it falling forward onto his forehead. When he turned to say a few words to the woman sitting next to him, I saw he had olive skin and a dimple, or it might have been a wrinkle, on the right side of his mouth. From the back, at least, he reminded me of a photograph of Mickey refereeing a recent high school soccer match in Biloxi that had appeared in a newsletter he'd sent me.

Our state senator, Jonah Golden, introduced Obama to roaring cheers. The white-haired man was clapping like mad. When Obama finished speaking, the man stood up and continued clapping. Then he looked at his watch and turned to leave. I knew in my gut it was Mickey.

I sprung out of my seat, turning to the man beside me. "Excuse me, sir. I need to leave now."

"Why? What's your rush? I don't know why the hell we gave you women the right to vote anyway. You belong at home watching the soaps. Running a country is men's work."

I let that pass and pushed by him. "Sorry," I said to the expressionless woman sitting next to him. "Sorry, sorry," I repeated as I managed to struggle out of the row without stepping on anyone's feet.

I kept a respectable distance behind the white-haired man, but didn't let him out of my sight. He had the same slight swagger in his walk that Mickey'd had as a young athlete. Maybe his brother-in-law lived nearby; maybe he'd been taken to the hospital or died; maybe Mickey hadn't visited him at all.

Or maybe it wasn't even Mickey.

It didn't matter, because I lost him in the crowds that had listened to Obama on the loudspeakers outside, those who had not been able to get seats. Mickey, or the man I thought might be Mickey, had disappeared. I was disappointed and relieved at the same time. I walked back to my car and drove home.

The first thing I did when I got upstairs was check my computer. There were no messages from Mickey.

I needed to clear my head, so I went out to the walkway to get some fresh air. A Lexus was parked outside the building. A man with a shock of white hair was sitting in the car like he didn't know what to do. I watched him get out of the sedan, walk a few feet, and then go back to the car. Though no one was with me, I blushed.

"How did he know how to get here?" I wondered aloud. "Did he follow me? Did he imagine that he saw me at the rally the same way I recognized him?"

"Mickey?" I called to him.

He got out of the car and looked up.

At first he looked shocked. Then he looked excited.

"Stay there, just stay there. I'll park the car and find you."

I watched him pull his car into a guest spot, rush towards the entrance, and disappear into the elevator. He was still a handsome man.

I stood mesmerized until he reached me, and I let him hold my head in his hands. "I've imagined for years how you'd look. I can't take my eyes off you. You're still as beautiful as you were then. My father always wondered why I let you get away—not that Judith wasn't a looker, but she didn't have your class."

"The neighbors, especially the crone next door, are probably watching us." I smiled. "Let's go inside." I took his hand and we entered the apartment.

We were hardly inside when his arms encircled my waist. He held me close.

"Mickey, would you like some coffee?'

"Not allowed. I had an ulcer."

"Ice cream?"

"No thanks."

"How about we just talk? We have so much to tell each other."

"Later."

I didn't even notice the red splotches on his arms, the hearing aid in his right ear, or the limp when he walked. All I saw was a young soccer captain…and he was leading me into the bedroom.

The blinds I'd lowered earlier in the day had kept the room cool, dark, and inviting. I felt like I was fifteen again, and Mickey was eighteen. While he kissed my mouth, my ears, and my neck, I managed to slip out of my clothes and let them drop to the floor. He did, too, and left his shoes at the side of the bed. I didn't bother to remove the quilt. It was the romance of the cheerleader and the soccer captain—he discovering, she enjoying being discovered. Together, we finished what we'd left unfinished forty years ago.

The following morning, I awoke to an empty bed, but the shower was running in the bathroom. A small suitcase sat on a side chair in the room. I guessed that Mickey had awakened earlier, gone down to the car, and brought up his clean clothes and toiletries. I pretended to be asleep until he came out of the bathroom.

He bent over me and whispered, "Glo, it was a great night."

"Do you want to make love again? Or shall I make us some breakfast?"

Mickey crawled into bed with me.

"Is it possible to love two women at the same time—one you never had but always imagined, and one who's been a good wife and taken care of you when the chips were down and you nearly died?"

"I don't know. Right now I'm free. If I ever love again, I'll want it to be like fireworks on the Fourth of July."

"Honey, I'll be glad if I can repeat last night's performance. You seemed to enjoy it."

It didn't take much foreplay before we proved that age was not a problem that morning.

I cooked some scrambled eggs and toast and carried the plates out to the terrace. We ate our breakfast slowly; the fountain in the middle of the lake added a romantic touch.

"How long can you stay?"

"I have to get back to Mississippi tonight. There's a big poker tournament at the casino tomorrow."

"Your brother-in-law?"

"We buried him early yesterday morning. I arrived in Fort Lauderdale in time for the funeral, paid my respects to his widow—Judy's sister—and drove up to hear Obama. I couldn't decide whether to call you or not. I knew there could be complications. But then I saw you and couldn't stay away."

"So what happens now?"

"Judy and I once filed for divorce, but never finalized it."

"Any reason?"

"It was easier to go on living together, and less expensive than living apart. Anyway, I had enough freedom to feel comfortable."

"You're so blasé about the whole thing. Over forty years and you show no emotion."

"Marriages come and go. Why don't we start e-mailing each other again and see what happens?"

The doorbell rang before my anger showed. I got up to answer it, ignoring Mickey's last statement. Opening it a mere crack, I saw my neighbor holding my newspaper.

"I got worried about you. It's ten-thirty in the morning already and your paper was outside. No tennis today. You didn't tell me you were going away nor had weekend company."

"Thanks, Mrs. Feingold. I'm all right. Just overslept. I'll take the newspaper. Have a nice day."

I didn't let her even peek into the apartment. Mickey was none of her business.

Returning to the terrace, I handed the sports section to Mickey and, out of habit, glanced at the front page. There, glaring at me from the front page was the headline:

New Rev Breaks Out in Haiti
Ex-pats Urged to Return Home

I wondered what Henri was thinking when he read the same headline.

Mickey was totally absorbed in the sports section, checking off the Sunday football games that interested him.

"I'm going into the bedroom to call my bookie. Is that all right, Glo?"

"Sure. Hope you pick some winners."

It gave me a chance to read the article about the political upheaval in Haiti. I recognized the name of the aspiring prime minister; a woman with the surname Betencourt. Was it his sister, or maybe a cousin?

Mickey came back to the porch, a grin on his face. "What are you reading?"

"Nothing important...just an article about the usual revolutions in Latin America."

Mickey didn't care and asked for no further details. He looked at his watch.

"That's it, baby. Got to go."

We both walked into the living room.

"Where's your suitcase?"

"Left it in your bedroom...until the next time. Will you wash my underwear?"

I thought he had a lot of nerve, but I ignored his conceit. "When do you think you'll be back?"

"Don't know. But I can't miss the four o'clock flight to Biloxi. I need a good night's sleep before the twelve-hour state poker championship. It starts at noon tomorrow with a $5,000 buy-in and a $50,000 first prize. Didn't I tell you about it?"

"No, I thought all along that you were an amateur. How will I know if you win?"

"Check your e-mail regularly. We get bathroom breaks."

He took me into his arms and kissed me hard, but I sensed he was anxious to leave. I'd made him feel like a real man last night, but I couldn't compete with four aces. I walked him to the door, watched him pull out, and waved goodbye. He blinked his brights in return despite the daylight.

When I was little, my mother made my father stop playing cards because he was away from home too much. She was right. To a gambler, a hot game is more exciting than a hot woman.

I desperately wanted to call Henri, but I didn't dare. It's something a Haitian woman didn't do, although the *moun gason* had all the freedom they wanted, including many women.

I was restless. I reread the article about Haiti and watched the news on TV; nothing new since this morning. I practiced memorizing a few phrases in my English–Haitian Creole Dictionary. Then I went to bed. Mississippi and Haiti merged into one tumultuous landscape: coconut palms, heavy rains, and mudslides surrounded the images of two men who had gone home for different reasons.

The next morning, I refrained from opening my computer until the afternoon. There was only one message:

From: Papmick@hmail.net
To: Globaby@eol.com

Dear Glo:

Taking a break (that's allowed, but not too often). Winning! Must be the inspiration you gave me in the bedroom. If I come in the top three, I'll stop at Ziff Jewelers. The owner's a buddy of mine. What about a diamond belly-button ring? Just kidding. I saw some blue-white sparklers for your delicious earlobes. Real diamonds. Keep the computer on. I'll check in again at the next break.

Lots of Love,

Mickey

Mickey had used the casino computer. There was no way I could send a reply to cheer him on; a flush or full house would do the job for me.

I had time before I had to get to my class and meet with Henri. I called my friend Joyce, and she met me at the local Dunkin' Donuts. Her boyfriend was a gambler, too. He'd abandoned a wife in Ohio, and Mickey had a wife in Mississippi or Georgia or wherever he'd last left her. Was it better than being alone? Is that why she and I had each started an affair in the first place? We finished our lattes, but came to no conclusion.

Dr. Pierre Betencourt was waiting for me when I reached the library.

"Hi, Glo! Surprised?"

"Yes, I am. Don't you have office hours today?"

"All the patients were pretty healthy. No emergencies."

I grew nervous and started scratching my hands. "Is Henri all right?"

"He's fine, but he won't be coming to class today. He flew to Haiti in a friend's private plane loaded with food and medicines. I don't know when he's coming back."

"I'm not surprised, after reading the papers yesterday. What does he hope to accomplish?"

"Henri is a humanitarian, as well as good soldier. He attended military school in France, and he's determined to see the revolution succeed."

50

"He never told me he spent time in France. No wonder he speaks French fluently."

"His cousin, who's destined to be the new prime minister, will need all the help she can get. Ours is a political family. And there's not enough money in the country for grain to feed the insurgents, let alone buy guns for an army."

"Will it be an all-out war?"

"All the international promises of aid were just that— promises. Henri knows how to raise money from successful Haitians, like me and other ex-pats. He makes us feel guilty about running away from poverty and making lots of money in the United States. Our old friends still have outhouses."

"Will he really be coming back?"

"He'll deliver supplies and funds to honest Haitians, who will distribute them to the needy. And then he'll come back here for more. In fact, he left something for you." Pierre took a letter out of his jacket pocket and handed it to me.

"Read it when you get home."

I started opening the letter.

Pierre stopped me. "Henri would prefer you read it when you get home. I think it is private."

Although the Betencourts had been polite to me at their daughter's party, they'd not been particularly warm. This time, Dr. Betencourt hugged me. He exuded the same masculine scent as Henri; they probably used the same aftershave lotion.

ঌ *Chapter Six* ঌ

The moment I got home, I opened the letter from Henri with trembling hands.

My dearest teacher, Gloria,

By now you know that I am back in Haiti and although there is much to do I am suffering from mal damou...*love sickness, I think you say in English. I am sorry that I missed today's lesson, but I miss you more. Perhaps today you brought a list of words of love instead of good things to eat. The heart is more important than the stomach.*

I'm sorry that I had no time to become your amourez *(lover I think?), but my country is bleeding, and I must help stop the hemorrhage with the older and wiser Betencourts who believe in honest government.*

The village where my wife and children died has been burnt to the ground by men who called themselves guerrillas, but were nothing but rapists and murderers. We need roofs above our heads before the heavy rains come. We need schools and a village square where men and women meet to sing, dance, and love again. If I die trying to bring peace and happiness back to my village, and my country, I will almost be a happy man.

Once upon a time, you would have loved it here, before the madness started. Banana and mango trees and coconut palms surrounded the edges of the village. Fish filled the waters surrounding Haiti's half of the island. Community plots of okra and sweet potatoes grew behind rows of flimsy houses. Almost everyone was poor, and many were barefoot, but no one was hungry.

If my cousin Michelle wins, I will probably be appointed minister of finance or minister of education.

What are you busy doing? A man without a woman is incomplete. There is an empty building down the road from my old house that would make a perfect schoolroom when it can be rebuilt. The village children need to learn about their culture and the rest of the world. They need an education. And I need to love a woman who understands my needs and respects my people. Is there any chance you might join me here when we regain power? Revolutions in this country are short-lived. I hope we will be victorious very soon.

My heart is filled with amore...*but my arms are empty.*

You can reply to me through Pierre. When it is safe, my brother can make arrangements for your flight...that is, if and when you are ready to come to me.

Your lovesick student,

Henri

I reread Henri's words several times. I thought about the shock of his sudden departure, the emotions expressed in his letter, and the feelings for him that I had thought would disappear as he succeeded, like his brother, in the United States. He was still young enough to start a new family. I was not. This relationship was insane.

On the day Barack Obama was elected president of the United States, Michelle Betencourt was sworn in as president of Haiti. Her predecessor and his followers fled the country and took whatever money they could get their hands on with them.

But the Haitian community had its own pipeline to Port-au-Prince. An orange flyer appeared under every door in their West Palm Beach neighborhood. It announced:

Michelle Betencourt New President of Haiti

Michelle Betencourt, a popular judge, has been sworn in as President Pro Tem of Haiti until the next election. Former President Joseph Oamunu and his henchmen were routed during the night by forces led by General Henri Betencourt, cousin of the new leader. The traitors fled to Panama. Extradition proceedings have been started to have the corrupt officials returned to Haiti to stand trial for absconding with treasury funds and stealing food and medical supplies donated by Floridian countrymen intended for distribution to their starving relatives.

Volunteers printed issues of *Libete* twenty-four hours a day in an unobtrusive gray shed behind Dr. Betencourt's office in West Palm Beach. The doctor continued taking care of his patients.

One of my students brought me a copy of the flyer. It had been weeks since anyone had seen or heard from Henri.

By now, the poker tournament at the Gulf Coast Casino had ended, but Mickey had not telephoned or e-mailed me. Either he'd been so busy winning that he refused to leave the poker table for more than a moment, or he'd lost so badly he was humiliated and holed up in his Biloxi house.

The short-lived revolution in Haiti had also ended. Dr. Betencourt delivered no further letters or messages. Henri, I assumed, was so busy balancing budgets or building temporary classrooms for his country's visionary future that he had no time to write. Or maybe a young, nubile Haitian girl had captured his admiration and satisfied his body. I was not certain that Dr. Betencourt approved of my relationship with his brother.

I skimmed Sunday's newspaper. There was no mention of Haiti in the international section. There was no mention of the $50,000 Biloxi poker tournament in the sports section, which had now added a page on gambling to its more traditional coverage. The winners were treated as celebrities.

I skipped to the crossword puzzle to abort my fantasizing. I reached eight-across—language spoken by Haitians. I smiled and had just entered *CR* when there was a loud knock on the door. Whoever it was had probably rung the bell, but it didn't always work.

I peered out the kitchen window. To my surprise, there stood Mickey. He looked haggard and old. I knocked on the window. His gaze shifted and met mine.

"Just give me a minute," I mouthed.

I hastened into the bedroom, ran a brush through my hair, and slipped out of my faded pajamas and into a flowing, floral caftan.

Mickey knocked again, this time even harder.

"Coming!"

I opened the door to a tired, white-haired man with bags under his eyes. He looked like he hadn't slept for days. In his right hand, he carried an overnight case; in his left was a small box, gift-wrapped in silver foil and tied with a shimmering satin ribbon.

"I'm beat," he said, walking into my apartment.

I had expected at least a hug. "Is that all the welcome I get?"

"Here, this will have to do until I get some rest."

He shoved the box into my hand and headed straight for the bedroom. There, he kicked off his loafers and lay down on the bed without disrobing.

"You didn't call me. I was beginning to think that you were never coming back."

"Sorry, baby. Lady Luck was riding with me. I haven't slept for days. Gamblers don't stop when they're on a winning streak, except to go to the john."

Then he closed his eyes. In a few minutes, he was snoring softly. His overnight bag dropped to the floor. I was left holding the beautifully wrapped box.

I went into the kitchen and sat down at the table. My hands shook as my fingers savored the softness of the elegant ribbon. Then, with one pull, I untied the ribbon and tore off the wrapping paper, revealing a small gold box. Ziff's Jewelers, Biloxi, Mississippi, was inscribed on top. I lifted it off and there were two diamond studs, each about one carat. No note, but I remembered what he'd said: "If I win, baby…"

I knew the way Mickey thought. The man had won $50,000 and the gift of the diamond earrings made me his…anytime, anywhere. All he had to do was show up, and I'd be ready and willing to take him in.

I went back into the bedroom for his bag, a duplicate of the one he'd left on his last visit. It was filled with wrinkled underwear, shirts, and socks. I transferred the new batch of soiled laundry to the washing machine. After all, I knew he expected some gesture of gratitude for his generous gift. As the machine began to churn, I took a look at the tags on the bag. The airline tag was dated, showing that it had arrived in Florida, via Georgia, several days after the tournament ended. Where had he been between playing poker and coming here? Had he stopped off to see his wife and granddaughter in Atlanta? There would be time to ask questions later.

Meanwhile, I slipped the earrings on, closed the French backs, and admired them in the hallway mirror. They were magnificent. It was certainly a gift Henri couldn't afford, but then…he wasn't here, anyway.

I kept returning to the mirror and admiring my new diamond earrings. But I was ridden with guilt. What was going on in Haiti? Where was Henri? Was he alive?

Mickey slept until late afternoon. I tried to read, started writing an undeliverable letter to Henri, and dusted my Lalique glass animal collection that had been neglected for weeks. Rescanning the newspaper, I found a small article about Haiti. Two gunmen had robbed a bank in Port-au-Prince, killed all the customers and tellers who were in the building, then escaped. No mention of a revolution. Henri had been a banker once, but…it was too crazy an idea.

There was a faint rustle at the door. Someone slipped an envelope underneath it. I rushed outside to the crosswalk and saw a black sedan with medical license plates pull out of a guest spot and speed away. It looked like Dr. Betencourt's car, the one I'd seen at the library. Could Henri be back in Florida?

I started to open the letter when the sound of the shower and a few off-tune bars of "Singin' in the Rain" distracted me. Mickey had obviously awakened and was washing off the gambler's grime. Like most ex-athletes, he needed to be squeaky clean once the game was over. And he'd always liked to sing.

It was hours since Mickey's arrival. I knew he'd be hungry for food—or sex. I wasn't sure in which order he'd be aroused, but I was ready for either.

I kept an auxiliary make-up kit in the second bathroom. A touch of cover-up, a hint of blush, and mascara…and the diamond studs lighting up my face. There was no need to change my floral caftan. It was a beautiful silk piece from India, and underneath it, I was bare.

It was too late for breakfast or lunch, so I dodged into the kitchen, took out a chilled bottle of wine, and made up a plate of olives, nuts, and cheeses. I might even broil a steak later, if Mickey was hungry.

I heard the sound of his electric razor. Perhaps I still had time to read the letter before Mickey demanded my attention. I curled up on the couch in the guestroom, far from the master bedroom. With trembling fingers I took the letter out of my pocket.

> *Dear Teacher,*
>
> *I never had enough sense to get your e-mail address, so I have to rely on my doctor-brother to be my courier. I'll be back in Florida in two or three days. I'm unsure how long I can stay. I don't want an English lesson, but I do want you. Pierre will let you know when and where. I've asked him to reserve a hotel suite for us. If you don't show up, I'll understand that, for you, it was just a middle-age fling. It wasn't to me. We Haitians aren't hung up about age. In fact, we admire the sensuality and wisdom that comes with it.*
>
> *My brother has secretly been keeping an eye on you. He thinks you have another man staying at your lakay. Is it true? That would make me very unhappy, because I love you.*
>
> *Henri*

"Gloria!" he yelled. "Come on in here. I'm wide awake and feeling hot to trot. Anything to drink?"

"It's on ice already."

I folded Henri's letter and slipped it back into my pocket. I returned the wine to the fridge, took a bottle of scotch out of the liquor cabinet, and filled a small silver ice bucket. I arranged the snacks, liquor, ice, and two glasses on a silver tray. Then I put a smile on my face and went to the bedroom. There he was, propped up like a pasha against the pillows, looking like he'd spent all his time in the sauna of a Palm Beach spa instead of a smoky casino. I wanted to laugh, but didn't want to offend him.

The muscles he had left were rippling, and his skin was smooth. He smelled of soap and aftershave lotion. A pair of navy blue boxer shorts covered his scarred lower torso where many surgeries had excised the cancers. The dimples of his youth were still there when he smiled.

"Honey, come here," he beckoned.

I put the tray on the nightstand, went to the bed, and lowered myself into his arms.

"You're still so beautiful," he told me.

His lips met mine; my mouth opened. His hands caressed my body and found the caftan's front zipper in seconds. He seemed pleased there was no underwear to remove.

"Lucky me," he said softly.

Mickey squeezed my breasts and played with my nipples.

He whispered, "Good, girl," as he licked my ear. I needed to be loved. I needed to return love. I knew Mickey was a gambler, a cheater. He had a wife he'd never totally leave. Only his granddaughter really mattered to him.

I slipped my hands into his boxer shorts and rubbed his penis, gently at first. He parted my legs.

"I missed you, baby."

He ran his fingers through my pubic hair until he reached my vagina. My lips grew wet and opened for him as he inserted his index finger. My insides grew warm and moist. The juices of love increased and mingled with his movements as he added a second finger and moved them in an up and down motion that turned me into his sexual toy. I couldn't resist his touch. He knew just which buttons to push. I grew wetter.

"All these years, I've dreamed about how it would have been if we had made love in the back of my father's car when we were young and wild."

"I'd probably have worried about saving my virginity through it all. There's nothing to stop us now."

"I love you," he said as he moved my hand so it rested on his penis and showed me what he wanted. My hand firmly encircled his manhood and moved up and down, as I covered his chest with quick kisses, until his member hardened.

We changed positions.

He lay over me, his chest propped up by his strong arms.

"What a woman you've become."

He entered me; our bodies became one. It wasn't long before we both climaxed. He held me in his arms, caressed my hair, and planted a series of kisses on my neck. We turned on our sides, looked into each other's eyes, and enjoyed the moment.

I'd never expected to hear from Mickey again, but fate had other ideas. Something about this guy had turned me on when I was a young girl and it still did. He knew it, too.

"Excuse me, honey."

He slid out of bed and went to the bathroom. When he returned, I was sitting up, covered by a sheet that ended just above my nipples.

"Mickey, why did you stop in Atlanta before coming to see me?"

He got back into bed, gave each of my semi-exposed breasts a gentle squeeze, and lay down beside me.

"It's not what you think. Judith traced me on her cell to the casino. She was frantic. Melissa tried to elope with Wilson, her black boyfriend. They stole her leased Lexus, took off towards South Carolina, and got into a car accident just north of the city. He walked away; she was hospitalized for two days with a minor concussion and a broken leg."

"What'd you do when you got there?"

"First, I went to see my granddaughter. I almost cried when I saw her bandaged forehead, black and blue face, and her leg in a plaster cast. We didn't talk about the incident. I just kissed her, held her hand, told her how much I loved her and that she'd get well.

"Then I went out to the dayroom to make some phone calls. I hired an aide to help Judith with Melissa when she's released, and called the police to report that Judith's car, the one in the accident, had been stolen by Wilson Boyce. They're looking for him now."

"Will he be arrested?"

"I hope so."

"Wow, that's some way to prevent a wedding."

"Let's go back to making love," he said, as he pulled the sheet down until my breasts were fully exposed.

❧ *Chapter Seven* ❧

I pretended to be sleeping as the rising sun peeked through the blinds, leaving a streak of sunlight across his handsome face. Mickey didn't know I was watching him; he'd picked up the remote from where it had haphazardly landed during last night's fit of passion, and clicked on the a.m. news.

It was a new day—another murder, another act of corruption, the weather and, unexpectedly, a news flash:

"Haitian military hero and Florida resident, Henri Betencourt, expected to return to Florida. Crowds of Haitians plan celebrations throughout South County in support of the Nouvo Pati Politik."

Mickey changed the channel.

"Go back, Mickey. I want to hear the rest of the news about Haiti."

"Since when do you care so much about that banana republic?"

"Many of my students are Haitians."

"They're probably glad to get out of that dump."

"The patriotic ones hope to go back some day."

"What for?"

I ignored the last statement.

"Time for breakfast, hon. Then I've got to do a little housekeeping, and I have students to tutor in the afternoon."

I bounded out of bed, heading for the shower, and then changed into shorts and a T-shirt. Mickey watched me the whole time.

"What are you going to do while I'm gone, Mick?"

"How about I make some calls, read the paper, and wait until you finish tutoring? Then you'll change into something glamorous and we'll drive to the Hard Rock Cafe. You know—dinner, dancing, the works."

"Tony Bennett's on the main stage tonight."

"He's older than us. I can listen to his disc at home. What about gambling? Practice on the video machines for a half-hour, and then I'll underwrite you at the blackjack table. You're smart enough to hold your own. The later the hour, the hotter it gets. Wear the diamond studs I gave you. They'll think you're a rich broad."

"They'll want to date me for my money."

"They'd rather see you hock them and keep gambling. But there's one condition."

"What?"

"Let me play poker at the high-stakes poker table alone for a while when you're comfortable with your game. Just kiss me for good luck first. I'll find you at the blackjack table or at the bar."

"Who knows who I might meet there? Don't you care?"

"Not my cheap Mississippi bible-thumping breakfast friends."

"Nor my hot-blooded Haitian students."

Mickey slapped me playfully on my behind. I went into the kitchen to prepare French toast. The day might turn out to be interesting, especially if Henri had really returned to South County.

I drove to the library on the outskirts of the Haitian neighborhood. It was early afternoon, but the parking lot was full of cars and crowds milling about. The double doors to the library were locked and a sign hung across them: Closed Today.

To my surprise, about fifty men and women, along with a few children clinging to their mothers' skirts, marched in front of the building carrying placards hailing Henri Betencourt as a hero of the revolution. Some of the women carried flowers. Was he in Florida already? Was he coming to the library?

The signs read: "Henri Betencourt Saves Haiti"; "Henri for President"; "We Want Henri, Not Michelle!"

A group of young girls carried a banner printed in red: "Stop Teenage Slavery." Other signs read: "Women Want Equality & Freedom Now!" Men's club members hoisted posters with pictures of voting machines and the message: "Permit Haitian Citizens in US to Vote in Your Election" and "We Love Our Homeland."

The chanting continued, growing louder. "Henri Betencourt saved Haiti; Henri for president; Haiti must become an honest democracy; let us vote!"

A black limo pulled up in front of the demonstrators. A group of young boys pushed me to the wall of the library, where I stood with other spectators watching a powerful, handsome Haitian in a general's uniform step out of the car followed by two bodyguards.

The crowd roared their approval. He let them shout for a while and finally lifted his arms into the air to get their attention. The voices ebbed, and then stopped.

He addressed them in Haitian, "*Zanmi, anmi...atansyon...*"

Then he repeated in English: "Friends, friends...attention...It has been a bloodless war, but we have driven out the tyrants who were robbing our country of its resources and money. Michelle Betencourt is returning from exile in Costa Rica."

The crowd booed. Some of them resumed their chanting: "We want Henri...Henri for *Prezidan*...Henri for President."

The general continued: "It is not important which Betencourt heads the government. Our philosophy is the same. What Haiti needs is change, and what it will get is productive change.

"First, the new government must root out corruption. Then we will start new industries with the cooperation of other countries, especially the United States. Our people are gifted with artistic talent. Collectors around the world are buying our tapestries and oil paintings. And there are enough Haitians in America to buy native cloth and works of art to decorate homes.

"Four to five million people are unemployed. Many live in the mountains. They trudge to the cities every morning to find a day's work, and are often unsuccessful. We must build roads and provide transportation so these men and women can reach the cities where factories will be built; not just in Port-au-Prince, but in Les Cayese and Limbe, in the mountains. South Korea and other Asian countries have expressed their willingness to invest in Haitian industries, and we must encourage their investments.

"But we must not destroy what exists. We must build on what is good in our culture. Even before we overthrew our French masters, Haitians believed in democracy. But democracy is only good when you have paying jobs, schools, and homes, and can see a doctor when you or your child is ill.

"We must help ourselves now. We cannot wait five years for the next election. I will be going back to Haiti next week to set up a new government."

"Viva, Henri! Viva Henri!" they shouted. The women threw flowers at him. The men raised fists and cheered.

The bodyguards cleared a path, and General Henri Betencourt walked to the entrance of the library. Perhaps he'd seen me leaning against the wall. I was glad I'd worn a dress with big, ostentatious yellow and orange flowers. I saw him notice me and smiled at him. Henri came closer and stopped next to me. Our arms went out to each other and we hugged.

In front of the marchers, he boldly kissed me on the lips.

The crowd grew silent and stared at us. Who is that white woman, they must have wondered. Papa Doc had had white women, but that was a long time ago and he was very rich.

"Sorry I can't stay for my lesson, teacher," he whispered. "Tropical Isle Inn, Bungalow number eight at ten p.m. Be there."

Henri walked back through the aisle to his waiting limousine. *"Bat bravo, bat bravo!"* the crowd cheered and applauded.

He was gorgeous, a natural leader, with a charisma that would attract any woman. Why me? My body trembled as I watched him drive away. His admirers scattered.

There would be no tutoring at the library today.

What would I do with Mickey? He was waiting for me at the apartment. We'd planned to go to the Seminole Café tonight to dine and gamble.

I needed a plan to cut the evening with Mickey short.

Both Mickey and Henri had aroused my libido, although their personalities were from opposite ends of the spectrum. Men, I know, dream of having a ménage à trois, but this was not my dream. Six months with each of them might be an ideal scenario.

I pulled into my parking spot. I had no patience to wait for our sluggish elevator and didn't want to run into any neighbors, so I ran up the four stories of side steps. Mickey had left the door unlocked, and I could hear him talking excitedly when I walked into the apartment.

"A thousand on University of Florida…Saturday's game, you moron…What difference does it make if the coach quit? Tennessee's a bunch of losers."

He turned, saw me, smiled, and ended his conversation. "Call you later."

"I'm home at last," I said and, walking over to him, kissed his forehead and headed for the bedroom. Mickey never asked me how my day had gone or if anything interesting had happened. He just followed me.

"I missed you, a lot."

Then he gently pushed me down on the bed and started taking his shoes off.

"What about a matinee, pretty girl?"

"It's four o'clock. That's tea-time," I joked. "I've got to shower and dress if we're going to the Seminole. You want me to look good, don't you?"

"You always look good." And he unbuckled his belt.

I remembered how ticklish he'd been when we necked as teens, so I reached out, found his ribs, and let my fingers do the talking. He lost his focus and laughed—the same giddy laugh of his young years.

I managed to slide off the bed and head for the bathroom.

"Put on a clean shirt, honey."

Once safely inside, I caught my breath and closed the door. I undressed and tossed out my clothes when I heard Mickey walk into the closet where he'd hung his suits. I turned the shower on full force and let the warm water wash away the lust Mickey had ignited in me. I had to make my plan work.

Wrapped in an extra-large bath towel, I came out of the bathroom.

Mickey was on the phone with his bookie again. "Georgia with ten points over South Carolina and Miami over Clemson by fourteen points. Five hundred bucks on each game. That's all."

I sneaked a peek at him. He was wearing a white shirt with thin blue stripes and looked very handsome.

By the time he returned to the bedroom, I had my black underwear on and was wearing a sequined, sleeveless top over a chiffon skirt with multiple knee-high slits around the bottom. The diamond studs were already in my ears.

"You look gorgeous."

"Except I can't close the back buttons. There are three up near the neckline. Will you help me?"

I turned my back to him.

The buttons were easy to find. The buttonholes were not.

He finally succeeded, but not before he slipped his hands under my blouse and fondled my breasts. I let him.

"It's good to have a man around the house."

"Dammit, you women, all these hooks and eyes, snaps or small buttons—when what we'd rather do is undress you."

The last thing I did was slip into my high-heeled patent pumps and grab a Peruvian black-wool shawl with an embroidered rose. I wrapped it around me, covering my bare arms against the chilliness I knew would pervade the casino.

Mickey took a navy blue blazer out of the closet, and we headed for the front door. Just when we were halfway out, I pushed him aside and quickly headed into the apartment.

"I don't feel well," I told him, and disappeared into the bathroom.

I pretended to throw up. I smudged my makeup and removed my lipstick; I dusted a little talcum powder over my face so I would look pale.

"Gloria, are you all right?" he called through the door.

"No, my head hurts, too."

"Don't take aspirin right away. You might not be able to keep it down."

"That's good advice."

I sat reading a *Martha Stuart Living* magazine from the stack that sat on the tank, flushed every few minutes, and sprayed the room with the air freshener. Eventually, I came out.

Mickey was pacing, looking at his watch.

"I can't go."

"Want me to stay home with you?"

"No, go gamble, Mickey. You'll miss it if you don't. I just want to get into bed. I'll take a rain check for tonight. Bring home the winnings."

"Are you sure it's all right to leave you here alone?"

"I'm sure. It must have been something I ate from the vendor's cart near the library."

He looked at his watch again.

"Okay, then, but don't wait up for me."

I heard the elevator take Mickey downstairs. Stealthily, I looked out the kitchen window and saw him drive away in his rented Lincoln. I smiled, went into the bedroom, removed my outer clothes, hung them up, and then stretched out on a pile of pillows to read Nora Roberts' novel *Unfinished Business* for an hour. When I put the book down, I figured Mickey would be deep into a poker game.

Then I dressed again. I thought my Haitian would prefer to see me in a simple white sheath with an accessible back zipper. The dress showed off my bare legs, high-heeled sandals, and red-painted toenails. I left the diamond studs in my ears. They gave my face the right kind of sparkle. Then I touched up my make-up and drove to the Tropical Isle Inn, where Henri was waiting.

The entrance to the Tropical Isle Inn is hidden from the street by giant red peregrina bushes transplanted from Cuba over a hundred years ago. The clusters of brilliant red flowers bloomed all year long and exuded an aura of mystery.

A gravel driveway cut through the dense vegetation to a small parking lot opposite the hundred-year-old main house, encircled by gracious porches. Usually a valet parks your car across the street, but tonight I parked it myself in a thirty-minute unloading spot, though I knew I'd be staying longer. All the restaurants were closed for the night. Only a lone drinker could be seen at the all-night tiki bar, its dim lights flickering through the porch louvers.

Lanterns hung from bougainvillea trees, casting eerie silhouettes on the small brooks stocked with multicolored tropical fish and electric eels. As I left the car, I heard a macaw calling to his mate and saw a monkey swinging from tree to tree. The tale of an adorable monkey who liked children and loved living in this environment studded with palms, bamboo trees, and other flora was now a community legend.

A blue moon lit up the tropical gardens; a sign pointed to the bungalows behind the historical house. I followed the path, passing gazebos housing romantic tables for two, set with linen cloths and candlesticks. When I reached the swimming pool, I could see the numbers on the bungalows. Number eight was the highest and the last in the A-section. A faux thatched roof accented its exotic look.

Laughter and Haitian music emanated from number eight. As I approached, a casually dressed couple came out of the bungalow. The young man wore a red-and-white silk shirt open at the neck, showing off a heavy gold chain with a clenched-fist fertility medallion hanging from it. He held the young girl around the waist with an air of possession. Henri was right behind them.

"Ou mesi," the young man said and kissed the taller man on both cheeks. His host returned their greeting and then went back inside.

I assumed they'd thanked Henri in Creole. The couple eyed me strangely; the party was ending and they were leaving, but I was just arriving.

A conch-shaped knocker substituted for the traditional doorbell. When I banged it against the door, it resonated like a voodoo drum. To my surprise, Pierre Betencourt opened the door and recognized me immediately.

"Come in, Gloria. Henri has been expecting you."

"How nice to see you again," I stammered. I was glad it was too dark for him to see me blush.

"Henri and I have a few more documents to review before I leave. We are planning a new airport in Haiti."

"How exciting. Where is the money coming from?"

Pierre ignored my question. "You and my brother need to be alone. Fix yourself a drink at the bar. It's in the corner next to the kitchen."

I walked to the bar and poured myself a glass of tropical punch from an ornate pitcher decorated with painted devils. I added a shot of gin to give me courage. Pierre disappeared into the bedroom leaving the door open, which made it easy for me to look around the suite.

The living room furniture was mostly bamboo with plump, festive cushions. Huge pots of geraniums decorated every corner. A peek into the bedroom revealed a king-sized teak bed with a canopy and side curtains. I heard footsteps and turned back to my drink at the bar as Pierre came out, carrying his jacket.

"Stay where you are and enjoy your drink, Gloria. I know my way out. *Bon nwit*—goodnight, cheri."

Seconds later, Henri walked into the living room. The beard he'd grown in Haiti was gone. Clean-shaven and dressed in an orange golf shirt tucked into beige linen pants, he exuded confidence and seemed relaxed. I wasn't. He stopped a few feet from me and waited. I went to meet him. We kissed without a word, and he pulled down the long zipper on the back of my dress.

"I've missed you, my woman."

"I've missed you, too."

We kissed again, as he pressed my warm body close to his.

"Can you stay the night?"

I swallowed hard, but managed to say, "Only until midnight."

"Then we have no time to waste."

The canopied bed was beautiful. Henri was a man of few words, but his hands caressing my eager body said it all. He knew how to excite a woman; well, he certainly knew how to excite me.

We left the curtains open so the blue moon lit our lovemaking and bore witness to the explosion of passion when it came.

It was warm and comfortable in the bed, but the flashing of the digital clock radio kept me aware of the time. At eleven-thirty, I slipped out of Henri's arms and left him sleeping, found my abandoned dress on the floor, pulled it on, and left the bungalow. I forgot my underwear in my rush, and I wasn't about to go back for my bra and panties—no one would see me on the deserted streets. I drove home quickly.

To my relief, my apartment was dark and Mickey had not yet returned. Hopefully he was winning and would stay at the tables until his luck ran out. I got into a terrycloth robe and dialed Henri while there was still time for us to talk. I wanted to hear him say he loved me in English. Earlier, in the big bed, I think he told me that in Creole.

His sleepy voice answered on the first ring. "Hi, my *amoure*!"

"How did you know it was me?"

"Who else would call at this hour after deserting me in this big bed?"

"You know I had to go. I'm sorry we didn't have time to talk."

"You said everything I wanted to hear with your body."

I pretended not to understand his sentiments. "Pierre mentioned the possibility of a new airport. Is it true?"

"We're negotiating."

"I'm excited for you. Will it replace the old one in Port-au-Prince?"

"No. It will be in Cap Haiten, to the north. That city can't stay isolated in the mountains; it has to be connected to the rest of the country. The women know how to sew, so the Chinese have offered to build a factory there if we provide an airport. It would also be a great port of call for the right cruise line."

"Who's paying for it?"

"Venezuela, maybe."

"Why? Have you discovered oil? I don't trust Chavez."

"Neither do I, but one never knows. He and I can talk. Royal Caribbean Cruise Lines is showing interest, too. I have an appointment to see their president this afternoon."

"Does Mr. Isaacson speak Creole or French?"

"My English is okay. *Ou mesi*…you taught me good."

"If *ou mesi* means thank you, then you are welcome."

"What are you doing later this afternoon?"

"If you're still at the Tropical Isle, it might be a good idea if I get my underwear back."

"Only if we have dinner first."

"It's a deal. How come they're sending you to negotiate?"

"I'm a good talker."

"You're a great lover."

"In Haiti, a politician has many jobs. By the way, what's your e-mail address? In some parts of Haiti, I can't use my cell."

"You mean you're not sending your messenger, Pierre?"

"My brother doesn't need to know everything."

I was lying face down on the big bed, fondling the receiver as if it were a part of Henri's body, and thinking how much I missed his touch.

Before I could say anything clever, I glanced at the television set. I'd apparently pushed the mute button on the remote, so there was no sound. But to my horror, buildings were toppling, people were running about in pajamas, IVs dangling from their arms. I turned on the sound, heard the hideous cries and saw the bleeding bodies.

Henri screamed, "An earthquake has just hit Haiti. The country is in chaos. I'll reach you later."

Dazed, I returned the phone to its cradle. A moment later, I heard a key unlock the door. Mickey was singing "First Love." He'd probably won at blackjack and had been drinking to celebrate. I ducked under the covers without taking off my smudged makeup and pretended to be asleep.

Without looking at the screen, he shut off the TV and took the remote out of my hand. He smelled of sweat and stale liquor.

I threw back the covers, sat up in bed, and looked at Mickey in disgust. Before I could control my feelings, I turned on him and yelled, "Henri's world is being destroyed and all you care about is a deck of cards or a crap table. Put the TV back on. I want to see what's happening in Haiti."

"Who the hell is Henri?" he said, and handed me the remote.

I didn't answer him, but resumed watching the horror of buildings toppling to the ground. Unwashed and fully clothed, Mickey lay down on the bed and fell asleep.

I watched shacks sliding down a mountainside and bodies being buried under mud. My heart was with Haiti and Henri. I wanted to comfort him.

I tried to call Henri back. The line was busy.

❧ Chapter Eight ❧

What if Henri was trying to call me? I stopped calling him, tucked my cell phone into the pocket of my terrycloth robe, and fled to the guest room. Mickey was snoring so loudly that he didn't hear me leave.

Frustrated and unhappy, I turned on the ancillary TV. While watching more buildings crumble in the seaside resort of colonial Jacmel, I tried to read *The Boy in the Striped Pajamas*, but couldn't comprehend the words. I removed the quilted turquoise bed cover, wrapped myself in the blanket, and tossed and turned until my bones ached and the phone fell out of my pocket onto the floor. I left it there and, finally, fell asleep.

The next morning, Mickey came into the room carrying a glass of orange juice. He was dressed in clean clothes and smelled of aftershave and Listerine. His black overnight bag sat at the door.

"Here, drink this," he said. "You'll feel better."

He picked up my cell phone from the floor and handed it to me.

"You must've dropped this while you were sleeping."

I flipped up the cover, but there were no voice mails waiting. I drank the juice and acknowledged Mickey's presence with a nod.

"You look like you're packed and ready to move on."

"Yeah, I think it's time to head back to Biloxi. But first I have to straighten out my family problems in Atlanta. I understand Wilson took Judith's car and got into an accident. My dumb wife probably won't press charges because Melissa's in love. In fact, she'll probably give them the money to fix it."

"Mickey, the only reason you detest Wilson is because he's black. Short of murder, you can't stop them from getting married."

"I can try."

"I wish you luck. Will we see each other again?"

"Who knows? What we had in a few days, some people never have in a lifetime. You're everything I dreamed you'd be. I'll always treasure those hours."

"I'm sorry it hasn't worked out. In some ways, I wish it had."

"The news in Haiti is so bleak, be careful what you wish for."

Despite his inebriation last night, Mickey was a pretty smart guy. He picked up his weekender, kissed my cheek, and left. He never asked me again who Henri was.

I got out of bed and checked my inbox. The e-mail I'd been hoping for was there; Henri had probably sent it through his iPhone.

From: Haitianman@net.il
To: Globaby@eol.com

My dearest Amoure:

Pierre and I emptied every 7-11 of bottled water from Lake Worth to the airport. My friend, Joseph the famasyent, collected antibiotics off the shelves of all the famasies—you call them pharmacies—from here to Miami. A crew of illegals loaded the aircraft, leaving just

77

enough room for the pilot, my brother, and me. There were no lights on the runway from which we took off. A box of syringes is poking into my ribs. I will reach you again as soon as I can. If you really care for me, pack a suitcase with just the essentials and be prepared to join me. Meanwhile, practice your Creole. I'll need your help and your love to get through this nightmare.

I love you.

Henri

I read the message over and over before I walked out the door to get the newspaper. The front page showed a woman, half-naked but alive, being pulled from the wreckage of a hotel with a dead baby on her breast. My tears flowed down my smudged face like the dirty aftermath of the mudslide on page one.

I went back to the master bedroom, showered, and got into a pair of dungarees and a sweatshirt. I attacked my closet with a vengeance, throwing clothes I hadn't worn lately into an empty cardboard box, and even included a few new pairs of shorts that still had price tags on them. I remembered that the fire rescue unit near the All Souls Church in Delray collected clothes for the poor in Haiti even before the earthquake. I could not bear to see the indignity of the earthquake's victims with their shredded garments, those injured bodies, the dead children. I rushed out the door, got into my car, and drove downtown to deliver the box.

Tonight, I would pack a suitcase for myself.

Twelve days had passed since nature unleashed the earthquake that nearly destroyed Port-au-Prince and its environs. I functioned in a daze, knowing Henri was there amidst the ruins and dead bodies, the spread of disease and constant hunger, struggling to save anyone he could.

My updates on Haiti came from TV, the newspapers, and my students. All of them had relatives in Haiti; some had been saved, though many had perished. They were desperate for some kind of closure. A few of the younger ones had not shown up for tutoring; rumor had it that, legally or illegally, they'd gone back to look for loved ones. Bodies needed to be buried so as not to incur the wrath of the voodoo Gods. Although I knew some of the students were acquainted with Henri, no one mentioned him or Pierre.

There were no messages from either Mickey or Henri. Mickey could be anywhere there was a poker tournament or crap game, and I wasn't sure when he would contact me again. I knew Henri was probably in Haiti. Even if he'd airlifted a few wounded to South Florida hospitals, he probably refilled his plane with supplies and immediately returned to help the hopeless souls sprawled over the streets of Port-au-Prince. He didn't have time for me, and I guessed I'd only be in the way.

But my suitcase remained packed and ready to travel.

The destruction, hunger, and humiliation of an entire nation had captured the attention of the world. The earthquake, it was estimated, had killed 150,000 men, women, and children. Only a few hundred had been rescued. Thousands of children were now orphans, and one million persons were homeless. The chance of saving more lives grew increasingly remote.

Although the Red Cross, Food for the Poor, Doctors Without Borders, and dozens of hastily organized groups were sending food, medicine, and manpower, no one remembered tents. It was hot and dry now, so refugees were using bed sheets, plastic wrap, tablecloths—anything that could be connected to four poles would serve as a shelter. But the rainy season would soon be upon them, turning the campsite in front of the wrecked National Palace, Haiti's White House, into a massive disease-infested swamp.

The latest newspaper photos showed chaos in the streets of Port-au-Prince. When relief agencies distributed food, the strong stole from the weak; teens ripped rations away from children and the elderly, and men overpowered women to get something to eat. A bowl of rice or a few crackers could be sold on the street for as much as a fourteen-karat-gold ring. Though supplies were reaching Haiti, there seemed to be no organized way of distributing them.

On this morning, my eyes found an article about South County schools planning to dispose of portable classrooms because the student population of Dade, Broward, and Palm Beach Counties had declined by several thousand in the last few years. A light bulb went on. I knew how to help Henri and the children of Haiti. I had an idea for how to bring some order to the tent cities that would be springing up all over the country. But where to begin?

I phoned Ellen McCoy at the literacy agency. She'd been my mentor when I first volunteered to teach English to the Haitian immigrants, and was also one of the founders of the agency. We'd met again at the coming-out party for Dr. Betencourt's daughter. We'd talked about everything from new theories for teaching immigrants how to read English, to the latest fashions, and what's new in regional theatre. We liked each other right away. But, more importantly right now, was that Ellen knew everybody of importance in the county school district.

"Hi, Ellen. It's Gloria Simon. I need some information."

"Is that all? How about a hello?"

"Sorry, but it's rather important. I need to reach someone in the county school district who knows what happened to the portable classrooms that have been dismantled in the past few years. Or will we need them again?"

"We might, if there's a flood of incoming children from Haiti, but there are plenty of empty seats in our existing schools."

"That's not what I had in mind."

"Want to tell me?"

"Not yet. First I want to get some facts. Get me a name and phone number. You know how hard it is to reach the right person in a government bureaucracy. Call me back as soon as possible, please."

"This doesn't have something to do with Henri Betencourt, does it?"

"We'll talk about that later. Meanwhile, I'll be waiting to hear from you."

❦

I busied myself around the house, watering the geraniums and African violets that were blooming early. I needed to hear a human voice, so I turned on the radio.

A reporter was saying, "The search and rescue effort is now ending. No one is expected to be alive under any of the remaining debris. The recovery phase—the search for dead bodies—is beginning."

I started to cry. What then? Reconstruction? Maybe that was when Henri would need me.

The phone rang. It was Ellen McCoy.

"I've got information for you. A guy called Neil Gallagher is in charge of portables. Here's his phone number."

"Okay, I've got it. Go on."

"He was rather vague about where they were. He'd heard that Dade and Broward Counties were considering selling their surplus classrooms to Panama, but he wouldn't be definite. He hemmed and hawed about how expensive they are to ship. Call him yourself. Maybe he'll be more responsive to your request, since I can only guess what you have in mind."

"Thanks, Ellen. Do you think Dr. Betencourt could enlist one of his ship-owner friends to donate a freighter and a crew?"

"I think I know what you're thinking now, Gloria. It's possible. He knows every Central American with money in the banana republics."

"If we can get the portables—if Florida will donate them—we can set up schools in the tent cities. The children will be busy learning while the adults will, hopefully, be rebuilding. Also, the makeshift classrooms could be used to distribute food and other supplies."

"Sounds like a great idea."

"Do you think Henri will think I'm interfering?"

"Go for it, girl. I think he'd be proud of you. But first, you'll have to deal with Neil Gallagher; he's a tight-fisted, stubborn conservative, and I'm not sure he gives a damn about Haitians. Let me know what happens. I would suggest that Dr. Betencourt use his influence in Tallahassee. He might know political honchos in the State Department of Education. I have an appointment—got to go."

"I'll call you later."

I turned on my computer. My inbox was full of unimportant messages, but there was one with a familiar address.

> *From: Papmick@hmail.net*
> *To: Globaby@eol.com*
>
> *Dear Glo:*
>
> *Forgive me. Don't you still want to stay in touch?*
> *I do.*
>
> *Love,*
>
> *Mickey*

I deleted the message and left the computer on standby.

❧ Chapter Nine ❧

For the entirety of the next day, I tried reaching Neil Gallagher, but the effort was fruitless. Either his line was busy or I was directed to voice mail, and he never called me back. Reluctantly, I telephoned Pierre Betencourt.

"Sorry, Pierre. I know the nurse said you were very busy, but I had to reach you."

Then I raced through the scenario about the portable classrooms, the inability to reach Neil Gallagher, and Ellen McCoy's suggestion that Pierre contact someone in Tallahassee, maybe a politico who needed the Haitian-American vote.

"No wonder Henri finds you interesting. By the way, I was going to call you after office hours. Be ready to leave on Thursday at four-thirty p.m. My chauffer will pick you up. I can't tell you where you'll be flying from, but Henri will be there when you arrive. They've opened a second runway at Toussaint Louverture Airport, so you won't be circling Port-au-Prince for long. You may be staying in Haiti for a while."

"What do I tell my family, my friends?"

"Tell them you're volunteering with Doctors Without Borders. We've arranged for you to tutor children at a makeshift hospital until we can start building schools."

"And the portables?"

"I'll get in touch with the Speaker at the capitol. Jose Colon is a friend of mine, even though he's a Dominican. If Neil Gallagher, that old fraud, hasn't sold them personally and shipped them already, Jose can put the screws on other representatives, and we'll get them. I'll let you know, or Henri will when you get to Haiti."

"Thanks, Pierre."

Several days later, a small private plane with two females and a lot of boxes on board glided to a stop on the second makeshift runway in Port-au-Prince, courtesy of the US Marines. I stared out the small windows and saw lots of bare-chested men directing the plane to its bay. Henri wasn't among them. I was simultaneously scared and excited at the thought of seeing him.

When the ladder was put down for us to exit the plane, the other person on the flight, a French Red Cross nurse, motioned for me to follow her. I gathered up my small suitcase and a tote bag of books and did as I was told.

There he was at the bottom of the landing steps, face glistening with sweat in the ninety-five-degree heat, a bouquet of wilting flowers in one hand, and his arms spread wide in welcome. I dropped my baggage to the ground and ran into his arms, ignoring the smell of death that permeated everything. The heat made our bodies stick together immediately, and it felt as if we were one. He cupped my face in his hands and buried it in kisses until our lips met. The ground crew looked at us, grinned, and then turned away, as if to give us privacy.

A young man in khakis with sergeants' stripes on his sleeve approached us, picked up my things, and addressed Henri. "Sir, it's time to go."

We let go of each other and followed the baby-faced officer to a waiting black limousine. The back was spacious. Once we were inside, Henri spoke for the first time. "I wasn't sure you'd come. In my stomach, I had butterflies all morning. Is that how you say it?"

I laughed.

"Correct me, please, if I'm wrong."

I moved closer to him on the back seat until our shoulders touched. "I've had butterflies in my stomach, too. Get it?"

"I get it. I am so happy you didn't disappoint me. It won't be easy, but we'll have each other."

"Henri, my love, I couldn't wait to get here."

"I've rented a small house for us on the edge of the resort city of Jacmel, ten miles south of Port-au-Prince. It has been cleaned and the walls whitewashed. Best of all, I've procured a big brass bed.

"The earthquake nearly destroyed most of the colonial-style buildings we inherited from the French. A school collapsed while students were beginning to prepare for Kanaval; the youngest and most vulnerable were injured or killed. Jacmel is littered with crumbling buildings, but it does not smell as badly as Port-au-Prince because of the sea breezes coming off the Caribbean.

"But our beaches are still lovely. When the rains come, wildflowers will bloom everywhere again and hide much of the damage."

I smiled at him and grasped his hand as tightly as I could. "I'll help in every way I can."

"Haiti is a tragedy. My heart is broken. We'll need all the help we can get to lift us out of this disaster. Some families are rebuilding already. We'll talk about what you'll do here in the morning."

"How do I say 'I love you' in Creole?" I asked.

"Mwen renmen ou," he told me, then kissed my neck and caressed my breasts.

We ignored the driver, and he, in turn, ignored us.

It was not until morning that I realized there were no shades to block out the blazing sun. Two children were peeking into our paneless windows. When they saw my nakedness, they giggled and ran off. But it was enough to wake Henri, and we both laughed as I slipped on an extra-large T-shirt he'd left on a chair.

Everything around me was unfamiliar, except Henri, who made no attempt to cover his nakedness.

"Kafi, my sweet?"

"Wi."

"There's some *pen ak friz konfiti* in the cabinet—I mean bread and strawberry jam. I've been speaking Creole mostly, but now that you're here I'd better polish up my English."

"Funny, I understood you. And I'd better practice my Creole. Is there any water for washing?"

"You have to get a basin from under the sink and go outside to the pump. We haven't had time to hook up the pipes. Don't feel embarrassed. No one's around."

I did as Henri suggested and when I returned to the house, the coffee had been brewed in an ancient pot, and the bread and jam sat on squares of salvaged waxed paper. I was a bit dumbfounded.

"It will get better, my cheri, I promise you. Doctors Without Borders is planning a temporary outdoor clinic for injured children on the beach. Many of them are traumatized. The warm sands will comfort them. The doctors want them away from the turmoil and horror of Port-au-Prince."

"How do I fit in?"

"You start working there today after I've shown you around the city. We live close enough that you can walk to the camp."

"Any pencils and paper?" I asked.

"Whatever I could collect is in the brown boxes I brought in when we arrived. My aides will take them to the site. The children will not arrive until tomorrow. Organize them into groups by age, I suppose; you know better than me. Start projects. Keep them busy. Some of the older boys speak some Pidgin English from hanging around the hotels where they did errands to earn a few coins. They'll help you until your Creole improves."

"And where will you be?"

"I have some important work to do in Port-au-Prince. I'll try to get back tonight and every night, although it might be late."

I looked around the house while Henri packed a few things in a knapsack. This time, a face was visible at the open window; a pair of jet brown eyes was staring at us. It was not one of the little boys from this morning, but a young, beautiful child-woman. When my eyes met hers, she turned and ran off.

❧

The children arrived in pickup trucks at noon the next day, each with a coarse rope around his or her neck from which a plastic tag hung. Some tags were yellow, others orange, and yet others green. The child's name, age, and parents' names were printed on one side of the tag; on the reverse was a diagnosis— trauma, leg amputation, unable to speak, bacterial infection, or general wounds. The identification side of a few tags read "Unknown."

I watched the French nurse, the one I'd casually met on the plane, spread straw mattresses on the sand. As the children were seated, an aide handed each a bowl of rice and beans and encouraged them to eat. Some did; others didn't. One or two deliberately spilled the contents out on the sand.

"Good morning, *enfimye*. Remember me?"

"Wi, of course. I'm Nadine. We met on the incoming plane."

"I'm Gloria. I'll be working with you. Henri Betencourt has suggested that I organize a temporary learning center for these children. I need to keep their minds occupied while you repair their bodies. He tells me that most of their schools in Port-au-Prince have been destroyed."

"That's unfortunate. Good luck."

"Do you mind if I regroup them according to age?"

"Just keep the ones with the same-color tags together. It helps us know what sort of medical attention they need. It's kind of a triage system."

"It would be better if there was some shelter from the sun—or the rain, when it comes, but nature is unpredictable."

"Tents are scheduled to arrive this week. We can only hope they do."

"I guess I'll wear my big straw hat and use lots of sunscreen. But first I have to recruit some of the older boys who speak English to help me. I made these posters this morning." In a rainbow of colored letters, I'd printed, "Do you speak English? I need your help. Come with me. It is OK with the nurse."

"Neat!" It was nice to see Nadine smile. She'd seemed so glum.

The signs worked. Walking up and down the rows of mattresses, I assembled half a dozen teenaged boys. Their English was poor, but it was better than my Creole. They followed me like I was the Pied Piper leading them to Nirvana, a place of painlessness and peace. I couldn't promise that, but I could promise them each an extra bowl of rice.

The sound of the sea had lulled some of the children to sleep, and I didn't wake them. I stopped at a group of children who all wore yellow tags, and held up papers and small boxes of colored pencils. That, and the teenagers trailing behind me, got their attention.

"Good morning children. My name is *Mis* Gloria. Today we'll draw pictures of the sea and pretend we're riding the waves on beautiful seahorses that will bring us home."

They looked at me as if I'd lost my mind.

Luis, the oldest of the boys, repeated what I said in Creole. Some of the children perked up, and another boy gave out drawing paper and colored pencils. A skinny tot put a pencil in his mouth and bit off the point, but one of my helpers stopped him before he swallowed it.

"Thanks, Raoul. That's one of the children who emptied his bowl of rice on the sand. Please see if you we can get him a couple of crackers. Ask for Nurse Nadine at the supply table. Tell her I sent you."

"Wi, Mis Gloria."

I nearly cried, but this was not a time for tears. It was a time for survival, a time for sympathy, a time for love. There was too much to do.

After a while we collected the pictures. The boys found some rope and, with two large sticks, built a clothesline in the sand. Since we had no clothespins, we hung up the pictures with safety pins borrowed from the nurse's supply room. My helpers made sure each child put a name on his or her picture. The children loved color, and the seahorses were gorgeous.

This was the beginning of our tent museum.

I let them chatter for a while, and was glad to see so many of them being children, even giggling, as they pointed at their pictures and at me. Then I gave placards to each of my helpers.

"Can you sing?" I said to the group.

My helpers repeated my question in Creole, and nodded. So did the other children.

"I'm going to teach you an easy song now. I'll sing it in English. It goes like this:

♫ We will get well,
We will go home,
We must find our families.
Haiti's our country,
By this beautiful sea,
By this beautiful sea. ♫

Then Luis sang it in Creole:

♫ *Nou pral byen,*
Nou pral Lakay,
Nou dive juen fanmil nou.
Ayitise peyi now,
Bo anpil bel lanme,
Wi anpil bel lanme. ♫

The boys went from group to group teaching the children the words, and suddenly they all started singing. Some of the children beat the sand as if it were a tin-can drum, adding rhythm to the sounds of their voices. The chanting grew louder and louder; the doctors, nurses, and aides stopped to listen.

Haitians, I began to believe, were a strong people. Perhaps there was hope for these children after all.

I couldn't wait to tell Henri about my day.

Exhausted, I drifted into a restless sleep, expecting Henri to wake me when he returned from Port-au-Prince. As I tossed and turned, a stream of questions cluttered my mind. Had I done the right thing by coming here? Could I give up my country for a Haitian lover? Suddenly Henri grew fainter, and then morphed into Mickey. I woke with a scream.

Henri didn't come back to the whitewashed house until almost midnight. He carried a laptop with him. He touched me and I awoke.

"Would you like something to eat, Henri?"

"*Non, merci.*" Sometimes Henri lapsed into French, which was often spoken among government officials.

"I'm so tired. Cabinet meetings lasted all day. With all these problems, there is still political squabbling."

"Maybe tomorrow will be better."

"I hope so. The mayor of Jacmel is my Uncle Rene. He's invited us for dinner. My Aunt Mimi is a great cook. Hopefully I'll get back early enough. If we're lucky she'll serve conch soup."

"Sounds delicious."

He kissed my forehead and cheeks, stretched out on the big bed without disrobing, and fell asleep. We had no time to talk about his day or mine.

I took the computer out of his hands and set it on the dresser. I wondered if it would be okay to check my e-mail messages. I'd better ask him if I could use it in the morning.

❧ Chapter Ten ❧

Tropical sunlight again ushered in the morning. There were no trees shading the small house. They'd been chopped down and used for fuel several years ago during one of the many uprisings. But someone had planted papaya bushes in the back of the house, and they were now bearing sumptuous, reddish-yellow fruit.

The bed was empty, and I was disappointed. But there was a note on Henri's pillow.

Had to be at work early so I can get back at 7 pm.

Love you, H.

His computer was not where I'd set it on the dresser. Nor was it in the kitchen. I wouldn't be able to check my e-mail or contact my friends and family, whom I missed already. I had the feeling that Henri didn't want me to; nor did he want me to see any personal information about himself or his country.

I arose, filled a basin of water from the outdoor well, and picked a ripe papaya for my breakfast. Because of the heat, I wore a pink sleeveless polo, denim shorts, and sandals, then smeared any exposed skin with sunscreen. The kettle whistled. I dropped several lemon-mint leaves from the garden into a cup of boiled water and let it brew. From a tin in the cabinet, I took a few *biskwit*, sliced the papaya, and started to eat.

There was a frantic knocking on the door and before I could answer it, Luis burst in shouting, "Come, Mis Gloria, the tents have just arrived! Hurry, you must show them how to build a schoolhouse just like the ones in America!"

He didn't wait for an answer or let me finish my breakfast. He took my hand, and we ran to the beach. A group of muscular men with sweat dripping from their headbands were unloading a huge truck that had made its way over the potholed roads from Port-au-Prince to Jacmel during the night. Native soldiers in khaki surrounded the truck to prevent theft.

The man with sergeant's stripes on his shirt raised a megaphone and spoke Creole to the children spread out all over the beach. Luis translated for me.

"Your tents have arrived. Any boys—or strong girls—over fourteen and approved by the nurse may help us assemble them. Each tent can hold six children with the same color ID tags. Tents can be hooked together to make larger spaces."

I lost my aides as they scrambled over to help the men unload, and then started assembling the tents by color. Some supplier had the knowledge and imagination to send them in yellow, orange, and green to match the ID tags. I hoped they were waterproof.

I approached the sergeant. "Do you speak English?"

He nodded.

"Can you connect three tents? I want to use them as a schoolhouse until portable classrooms arrive from Florida—if they do."

"Are you Mis Gloria?"

"Wi."

"I'm Sergeant Duval. I heard the children say that you are kind. You have made them feel that they are able to draw and sing

93

and still be children. I even saw a few of the saddest ones smile. Some laugh when you try to speak Creole, but they appreciate the effort. You have given them hope and that is good. I will have the men do anything you want. Any particular color?"

"Mix and match them. Make the tents colorful."

The sergeant laughed.

"Now, can you find me some blackboards?"

By the time evening fell, all the tents were assembled and the children had moved their sleeping mats into their assigned spaces by themselves or with the help of others. It had been fun sleeping on the beach under a full moon, but it was safer in a tent. And although their future schoolhouse looked terrific with its tricolored exterior, the inside was bare.

Before the truck left, the sergeant found me.

"Tomorrow or the next day, we will return and bring you tables and blackboards. We'll move them out of school buildings that are too unsafe to be used any longer. Aftershocks will make many existing walls crumble. But some still have furnishings, and if we hurry we can get them out. I'll get volunteers to help me when I tell them what you are doing here."

"Merci, merci, my good man."

"Just continue to love our children."

I shook hands with the Haitian sergeant.

"Why is a beautiful lady like you spending yours days on this decrepit island?"

"It's a secret."

Henri arrived shortly before seven o'clock. He parked a Jeep outside the front door and found me changing my clothes. He seemed tense and didn't bother to kiss me even on the cheek.

"Hurry, Gloria. *Tant* Mimi doesn't like it if you're late."

"I'm almost ready," I said as I changed into a simple yellow sundress. "I thought I'd check my e-mail before we go."

"What for? I'm here. Isn't that enough for you?"

"I have family and friends in America I'm not about to forget."

"Haiti is in America, too. Didn't you tell your American boyfriend that you'd be away for an indefinite period?"

I blinked, but didn't respond. There was no way Henri could have known about Mickey unless he'd had me followed from my tutorial sessions at the library. I managed to control my temper.

He splashed some leftover water from the basin over his face, then dabbed on some men's cologne.

"Meet me at the Jeep, Gloria," he said, and left the hut.

I silently brushed my hair, and went out to join him.

As Henri helped me into the Jeep, I saw a young woman lurking behind a pair of hibiscus bushes that were just beginning to flower a few feet from the door. It was the same face I'd seen outside our window the first night I slept at the house with Henri. When my glance met hers, she moved behind the bushes on the other side of the house, and I could no longer see her.

As far as I could tell, Henri's uncle's two-story house was just minutes away. It had not suffered at all from the earthquake.

"*Antre zanmi mwen*" said Henri's uncle. "Welcome to our humble house."

"Where is Tant Mimi?"

"In the kitchen. Where else should she be?"

Tonton Rene led us into the dining room. He was an older man with steel-gray hair and the bearing of a respected patriarch. The table was set with good silverware and china; not everyone had been wiped out by the quake. When we were seated, he served liqueur made from cherries.

"Come, Gloria, sit near me," Henri's uncle almost commanded.

I did as I was told.

"I understand you are teaching the children English."

"Yes, and they are teaching me Creole."

Aunt Mimi came in, hugged Henri, and chatted away with him in Creole since she knew no English. He followed her into the kitchen where he fixed her washing machine, an old manual wringer model. We could hear them talking while he worked. When they returned to the dining room, she embraced me like a long lost relative. Henri carried in a tureen of conch soup and she proceeded to serve.

The soup was followed by chicken that had been marinated in orange and lemon juice and accompanied by fried plantains. It was spicy, but delicious. Dinner ended with coffee and assorted fruits. I had never seen a *grenadye* before. It looked almost like a pomegranate.

"Henri, help Tant Mimi with the dishes. I want to have a talk with Gloria alone."

"Wi, Tonton Rene."

When the two left for the kitchen, the questions began.

"How old are you, Gloria?"

"Why do you ask?"

"Henri is only forty-one."

"Does it matter?"

"Yes. Can you still have children?"

"Probably not."

"You are a very beautiful woman and a smart one. I can understand why my nephew fell in love with you, but…"

"You don't approve."

"There's a young woman in the village who can give him many Haitian children. It would be better if you went back home. Henri has a great political future. He needs a Haitian wife and children."

"Is that what Henri wants?"

"We've talked about it."

"Is that young woman the one who's stalking me and peeking into our windows?"

"Maybe. Her grandmother was a voodoo priestess."

At that moment, Henri and Tant Mimi returned to the dining room. They were laughing. Henri put his arms on my shoulders.

"Come, Gloria, the washing machine is fixed, the dishes are washed, and it's time to go home."

"Au revoir," he said.

"Thank you for a lovely dinner," I added.

A full moon illuminated the debris and collapsing structures along the road from Uncle Rene's house to ours. It was as eerie as an Utrillo painting or a war zone decimated by an aerial bombing attack.

I sat as far away from Henri as I could without falling out of the Jeep. It was over ninety degrees, but I felt chilled.

The conversation with Uncle Rene left me confused and uncomfortable. Henri had not warned me about his uncle's disapproval of our relationship.

As we approached our small house, the Jeep's lights focused on a tall, slim, barefoot woman with her hair in dreadlocks. Despite the semi-darkness, a strapless blouse showed her cleavage, where a glittering cross on a silver chain hung between her breasts. For a moment, the Jeep's brights stunned her like a spotlight on a deer. She froze, a statue with a beautiful face—too young to be Henri's daughter, but not much older. Then she sprinted behind the house and crouched behind the papaya bushes. I could no longer see her, but for some reason, I felt inadequate. Henri pretended not to notice, or he hadn't seen her at all.

Once inside, I left him in the kitchen and went to the bedroom. I had a lot to think about.

He called after me, "Gloria, come back in here. I'll sign you on to my computer if it's so important to you."

"I'd rather use your laptop in the privacy of the bedroom, if that's all right with you."

He brought the computer to the bedroom, put it on the bed, and turned it on. I waited. Henri stood there watching me, waiting for me to sign into my e-mail.

"Henri, it's been a long evening. Why don't you go into the kitchen and have some tea? I need to be alone."

He scowled at me, and muttered as he left the room, "You *fanm*, no matter what we do, you can't please them."

I entered my e-mail address and password. In seconds I was staring at more than forty e-mails in the inbox that had accumulated over the past week. I deleted those from vendors, charities and self-help gurus. Five remained, and all were from Mickey. The subject line on each read "Urgent. Please Read Carefully."

Ignoring the first four, I opened the newest one:

Gloria, forgive me. I miss you. Judith is not coming back to Biloxi. She's moved into her sister's house in Atlanta. We've separated for good this time. I'm seeing a lawyer tomorrow. She's grown obese and boring and can't control our granddaughter anyway.

Wilson, Melissa's boyfriend, was released from jail since that lazy bitch Judith wouldn't press charges as long as she got her car back. And to think I got it for her on her last birthday. She'd rather file for divorce, she said, and I told her to go ahead and do it. Our marriage has been on the fritz for a long time.

Please get out of Haiti now. I'll be sitting on your doorstep as soon as I know when you're coming home. You belong in the good old USA and, hopefully, to me.

Anxiously waiting,

Mickey

I read that e-mail over several times before I rejoined Henri in the kitchen. We sat there, just staring at each other.

I broke the silence. "You're not hiding a printer somewhere in the house, are you, Henri?"

"No, but I'll print out whatever you want at the office tomorrow."

"Don't bother. I'll copy it by hand."

"It's from him, isn't it?"

"Yes."

"And I suppose you don't want me to read it."

"That's right. Why don't we talk?"

"About what?"

"The voodoo princess."

"Log off the computer, Gloria, and come sit beside me on the back porch. Did I tell you that my grandmother used to live in this house? There's an old double swing out there that I liked when I was a boy. I hope it's not too rusty."

"I'll meet you outside in a few minutes. I've one more message to read, then I'll put them on a disc and Nadine can print them for me tomorrow at the hospital. Would you like me to bring you a glass of lemonade?"

"Sounds good, I'm thirsty."

"And a thin blanket to spread out on the swing."

"A cotton sheet would be cooler, cheri."

He preceded me out onto the porch.

❧ Chapter Eleven ❧

I prepared a tray with two glasses of lemonade and took it outside. Henri took it from me and set it down on a rickety side table made of sugar cane stalks. I returned to the house for a clean sheet, folded it across my arms like it was a peace offering, and handed it to Henri. Without saying a word, he spread it across the swing's seat, sat down, and drew me between his legs.

I stood there motionless as he unbuttoned my shirt, unzipped my shorts, unhooked my bra, and pushed my panties down. I stepped out of them as soon as they reached my ankles. My body was overcome by desire, my flesh tingled, my knees grew weak. My breath quickened and I could hear the small gasps escaping from my lips. I let him caress and kiss me everywhere as if he owned me.

Moments later, Henri stripped off his clothes. It was a very warm night, and we came together as the swing sang its own rusty song, punctuating the stillness with a unique rhythm that somehow enhanced our lovemaking.

We never drank the lemonade.

Wrapped up in the security of his arms, I looked up at him and inquired, "Tell me about the voodoo princess."

"Lucia is just a young girl, but Haitian teenagers are more sensual than American girls. They need to be loved at an earlier age. Her grandmother was a *manbo*, a female priestess raised by

French-Catholic landowners whose estate adjoined the local cemetery. Her mother inherited the gift of casting spells and it is rumored that Lucia, too, has the power to raise the dead."

"Did you make love to her?"

"I don't want to lie to you, Gloria. The work was backbreaking. Clearing the debris of buildings, rescuing a few, and retrieving dead bodies traumatized my soul. Lucia was always underfoot trying to resuscitate the dead with spells that never worked. I needed the warmth of a live body. She was there."

"You didn't answer my question. Did you sleep with Lucia?"

"Yes, I did. In Haiti, it is not considered a sin for a man to have more than one woman. He does not marry all of them, although he may—or may not—acknowledge their children if they are his."

"And now that I'm here?"

"Don't worry. Haitian priestesses don't make voodoo dolls and stick them with pins to torture their rivals. The dolls are only made for the tourists."

"Was that supposed to be funny?"

"No, Gloria. I love you, I don't love Lucia."

"Are you going to stop seeing her?"

"I don't think that's possible."

"Why not?"

"She's pregnant."

I pushed my way out of Henri's arms and ran into the house, leaving my clothes on the porch floor.

Henri didn't sleep in our bed that night. I hardly slept either. The mattress seemed lumpy, strange birds shrieked all night and flew past the open window, the brushing of their wings across the outside walls making me shiver. The shadow of Lucia hovered over the bed, pointing an accusing finger at me.

Henri had not returned by the following morning. I had a feeling I knew where he'd gone.

I arose at dawn and returned to our tent city. The beach and the sea were serene. The children were still sleeping, although some of them called for their mamas. Others tossed, turned, and cried. A few of the older girls comforted the little ones.

I found Enfimye Nadine, as the children called her, in the service tent.

"Morning, Nadine. You're up early, too, and that's good because I need your help. I want to start teaching some of the children to read. I discovered that half of them don't know how; some have never been to school. And with most of the schools destroyed, who knows if they ever will."

"But you have no books, Gloria."

"But you have a copier. I've handwritten lesson one for the non-readers. Luis will be my assistant."

"Luis is only street smart."

"But he can read and write, at least phonetically; he can work with the older children who can read a little. They can write group stories as soon as the blackboards arrive, and learn from their own experiences. Most of the teachers in Haiti aren't too educated, either. Many have never gotten past ninth grade."

"And until the blackboards arrive, if they do?"

"They can write words in the sand with sticks."

"How can I say 'no' to you? Go, make copies. I'll show you where the machine is. Handle it carefully; I need it to duplicate medical records. The French Red Cross shipped it here and won't be anxious to replace it."

"Did they send a computer?"

"Two. I have a Dell, and Dr. Marchon has another in Puerto Prince; we must be able to communicate and share information."

I smiled at her. "You're a *bon zanmi*. I need to send a message to an old friend."

"Doesn't Henri have a laptop?"

"He doesn't have to know everything about me."

"Trouble in paradise, I presume."

"You're so right, Nadine. I'm not even sure I want to sleep at the house tonight."

"There's always an extra mat for you here."

"When may I use your copier and computer?"

"Now, before we get busy serving breakfast and meds."

I kissed her on both cheeks and went to the office at the back of the service tent to make copies of lesson one for the children.

Then I slipped the disc into the machine and reread Mickey's message. I started e-mailing a reply, but I wasn't sure what I wanted to say. I thought about getting out of Haiti. Perhaps Uncle Rene was right; I wasn't the woman for Henri. But Mickey might not always be waiting at my front door. I cancelled the outgoing message.

I needed more time to think.

My thoughts and feelings about Mickey were erratic. I recognized the flaws in his character, but there was nothing wrong with the way he made love. I wasn't ready to commit to any kind of relationship, but whatever I wrote had to be honest and come from the heart. Maybe his marriage to Judith should have ended long ago, but that wasn't my call. Mickey satisfied me in the bedroom, and made me laugh and remember old times. It was a nostalgic relationship mixed with revived physical pleasures. This was not the time to tease an old boyfriend.

Outside the tent, the children were giggling. I could hear the noise of crunchy cereal mingled with the words they wanted to share. It was hard even for children to chew and talk at the same time, but it was good to hear them laugh. They expected me momentarily. I'd spent too much time in the service tent mulling over my predicament.

Finally, I wrote.

> *From: Globaby@eol.com*
> *To: Papmick@hmail.net*
>
> *Dear Mickey:*
>
> *The heat is driving me crazy and I'm in emotional torment. I don't know what to say except that you were so right. I love the children, I love the Haitians, I cry for those who were buried alive and for those who now live with their despair. But I don't fit in.*
>
> *Henri is a brave, intelligent, and handsome man determined to revive his country, and he loves me. But he's not a one-woman man and I won't share him with a young brown-skinned beauty because she can bear him children. I couldn't be the other satisfied woman in a two-room hut where the mosquitoes never stop biting and the rainy season threatens to wash us all into the sea next month.*
>
> *Marriage is not important in this country. Polygamy without legal sanction is everywhere, and it certainly is not an option for Henri and me.*

Like you, I've been there. Married, borne my children, raised them, and allowed them to follow their own destiny. I love the young orphans I'm teaching here on the sands of the Caribbean. I'll continue to soothe their sorrows, hug them, and heal them until they're strong enough to survive in this insane, storm-tossed world. I know I'll come home again, I just don't know when. I know that I want to fly high and wide and see other corners of the world. I learned that here in Haiti. This is an insular country, and I do miss the comforts of home.

A few cases of malaria have surfaced and two very sick patients have been airlifted by helicopter to a special hospital in Port-au-Prince. There is no vaccine, but with preventive measures and the right medicine we'll all be all right. We're expecting shipments of chloroquine, insect repellant, and netting this afternoon; and maybe, if we're lucky, the blackboards will be on the same truck.

Sometimes I think I made a mistake about you. I knew I missed you when I read and reread your e-mails. I was sure I wanted to see you again. When you're not at the casino, you're a great guy to be with; but I must confess I don't remember loving you as much as you say I did when we were teens. You were afraid of getting serious and ran off to join the Navy, and I was practicing to be a woman.

Have you really separated from Judith? Is she filing for divorce—uncontested divorce? More importantly, have you stopped loving her? Do you still feel you owe her your loyalty because she stuck by you through an illness? That might be an eternity, more time than we have. I want to feel that we're both free to live and love. No encumbrances, no suffocating relationships, no regrets.

Is there an Eden we can run away to?

Love,

Gloria

As I prepared to push the send button I hesitated. Instead, I saved the e-mail as a draft and printed out a copy. Did Mickey really have to know so much about Henri? I didn't want to force either Mickey or Henri into an awkward position I'd later feel sorry about.

As I left the service area a delivery truck, escorted by military police on motorcycles, rumbled up the rut-filled road. Sergeant Duval waved to me from the window of the cab.

It would be a very busy day for all of us at this tent city.

❧ Chapter Twelve ❧

The truck stopped outside the tricolored tent-schoolhouse, and I could hear the commotion it caused among the children. I wedged a copy of the e-mail draft into the back pocket of my shorts and ran out to find the friendly sergeant who, I suspected, would supervise the unloading of the truck.

Luis and his helpers were already all over him. "Sergeant Duval, we're here, ready and willing to work. Just tell us what to do." The sergeant laughed, his big grin exposing gleaming white teeth. "Give me *dis minit* to check the inventory and I will get you boys to work."

Before I tapped the officer on the shoulder so he'd turn around and see me, I scratched my upper right arm. It had been itching all morning. *Those darn mosquitos*, I thought. I kept scratching until droplets of blood trickled down onto my hand. I had nothing to wipe them away with, so I just let the blood drip to the ground. Then I tapped the officer on the shoulder. "Sergeant Duval, you kept your promise. I'm so glad."

He turned to me and smiled. "You remembered my name."

"How could I forget your kind offer?"

The itching wouldn't stop. I scratched my arm again and more droplets of blood trickled down to my hand. I began to feel cold.

I saw the boys unloading blackboards from the truck. Behind the blackboards were boxes marked "chalk" and "erasers." Then things grew blurry. Sergeant Duval was looking at me strangely.

"Are you all right, Mis Gloria?"

"No. I'm so dizzy."

"You are so pale, madam."

"I don't know why but I'm so tired."

My knees buckled. I felt myself slip down on the ground. Two strong arms picked me up and carried me somewhere. My teeth started chattering.

I kept scratching the bump on my arm over and over again.

"Enfimye Nadine, Enfimye Nadine, come quick," someone yelled. "Our Mis Gloria is sick."

❧

The next thing I remembered was lying on a clean white sheet in the hospital ward of the service tent. There were other patients beside me. Enfimye Nadine was hovering over me, and had started an IV drip in my arm.

"What happened to me, Nadine?"

"You have malaria. You were probably bitten by an infected female mosquito."

"Will I be all right?"

"You're a lucky lady. Behind the blackboards and the chalk were boxes of anti-malaria medicines. It's the beginning of the annual epidemic here in Haiti. Quinine is going into your body right now."

"Does Henri know?"

"Not yet. Only the children, but I suspect the whole town will know by nightfall,"

"Tell them not to worry, I'll see them tomorrow. Let them practice the alphabet, sing silly songs, or dance. No swimming today unless they find a lifeguard. I can't watch them."

I realized I wasn't making sense, and so did Nadine.

"The fever is making you a little delirious, but you'll get well, my friend." Nadine wiped my forehead with a cold, white cloth. "It will take time."

The itching had subsided a little. I felt weak and cold, but my body was hot to the touch. I was running a fever and I was scared. I grew quiet. Nadine brought me some orange juice.

"Drink this. It will make you throat feel cooler."

"Thanks, my amie."

"Rest. You need lots of rest before you can even get out of bed."

"The e-mail, the e-mail! Where is it?" I suddenly screamed and bolted upright. "Henri mustn't read it."

"Ssh, lay back. I found it crumpled and dirty in the mud near where you and Sergeant Duval were talking. A lipstick and comb were lying next to it. The sergeant was so worried about you that he didn't bother to pick them up before he carried you here."

"I'm so glad nobody trampled it."

"Do you want me to send it for you? The e-mail address is quite readable."

"No, just hold it for me. But maybe you should let Mickey know I'm sick."

Nadine folded the draft and put it in the pocket of her uniform. "It will be safe with me. We'll discuss what to do with it in a few days when you are feeling better."

I could no longer stay awake. I shut my eyes as the quinine began to do its job.

That evening, I sensed Henri standing near my bed, holding my hand. In the morning, there was a pot of annua tea at my bedside. The patient in the neighboring bed told me that a beautiful young girl had delivered it about an hour ago.

"Drink it," the old woman said. "It's a Haitian cure for malaria."

Nadine told me a mild case of malaria lasts from two to three weeks. I was lucky. Even before the third week, the alternating sweats and chills and the fever grew fainter and disappeared. There were periods of delirium and periods of clarity. I tried to mark off the days I spent in bed on a notepad, but I couldn't keep track of them. I didn't remember if Henri visited me even once during that time.

One morning, the itchiness and illness ended. I awoke to a world of sunshine and the sound of the sea as the surf washed up on the beach. I tried to get out of bed, but I was so weak that my knees buckled and I wound up sitting on the dirt floor.

Lucia mysteriously appeared to help me up. The IV had been removed and a bundle of tropical flowers lay across my nightstand. She held me under my arm, and we slowly walked across the sand to the edge of the sea. The children stared at us, but continued to sight-read out loud from the experience charts I'd taught the English-speaking boys to make. Luis was a natural-born teacher and leader.

Some of the boys had left the school area and were attaching tarps to the canvas tents. Ominous dark clouds were moving toward us from the south, and that meant rain, heavy rain.

I tired as the waves washed over our feet, so we walked back to the service tent. Nobody wore shoes around here.

Lucia spoke to me for the first time, "Would you like some breakfast, Mis Gloria?"

"I think so. Mesi, Lucia."

She removed the flowers and placed them in a wicker basket on the floor. Then Lucia spread a white cloth across the nightstand and disappeared to the back of the tent. She reappeared in minutes with a tray of bread, jam, sliced bananas, and aromatic hot *chokola* made from the sweetest fresh cacao, the pride and cash crop of northern Haiti. Where this quiet girl had procured these delicacies amid the chaos of Jacmel would remain her secret. She placed the tray on my night table and moved on to help others near me.

I didn't remember when I'd eaten last, but I enjoyed the light meal she served me. I watched Lucia move about the tent. She was beautiful. Her long black hair reached her waist, and a purple flower attached to a hairpin kept a few stray curls behind one ear. Her skin was dark and silky, not a wrinkle to be seen. When she smiled, it was contagious and I couldn't continue to hate her because she had bewitched my lover with her grace and youthful body.

A small mound protruded under her flowered wrap-style dress. She was in the early months of pregnancy, but I saw Henri's face every time I looked at her belly. Lucia and I came from different times and different worlds. It would be impossible for us to compete for the same man on their native soil.

Meanwhile, messages kept arriving from Mickey. Nadine would print them out and bring them to me. Essentially, they all said, "Where are you, Gloria? With every passing day, I miss you more and more. Come home, I'm waiting for you. Love, Mickey"

A few days after the fever subsided, I was allowed to walk around the camp alone. As I got stronger, I began to supervise the learning sites under the orange and blue tarps. The blackboards, notebooks, and other supplies survived the scattered showers, but the bedding was soaked. The youngsters pulled them into the sun to dry. The puddles in the holes on the road that ran along the beach were also drying, and the mosquitoes were less active.

It was, however, an ominous sign of the torrential rains that would come in a few weeks. Preparation was important. We were short of tools. Men and women were using kitchen spoons and their bare hands to dig drainage ditches around their tents.

The ineffectual government had promised safer housing, but no relocation sites had been acquired. The older ministers seemed paralyzed in their offices, unable to take any decisive actions.

I saw Nadine waving a newspaper in the air as she raced towards me. She found me talking to Luis.

"Gloria, Sergeant Duval was here early this morning. I didn't want to wake you up. You still need rest. He dropped off supplies and this English language newspaper. Take a look."

I took the paper from Nadine's outstretched arm. There was a picture of Henri Betencourt on a crude podium, addressing a bedraggled crowd outside the lopsided, unrepaired National Palace. An unidentified woman with a belly stood off to the right of Henri; I thought it was Lucia.

"'Henri Betencourt declared himself housing minister yesterday," I read aloud, "and confiscated the highlands of the cacao plantation owners in the north.'"

"Oh, my God," gasped Nadine.

"Henri, the cousin of the prime minister, Michelle Betencourt, appears to have taken over the government and is desperately racing to provide permanent housing for the thousands of families living on the streets or in unsafe tents that will likely collapse when the seasonal rains arrive."

"Go on."

"Hunger and disease are increasing. Only inadequate food and a few medicines are reaching the makeshift settlements. Rape has surfaced as hungry, idle men look to escape the boredom of unemployment. The world is now focusing on other tragedies."

"I know," interrupted Nadine. "Rumor has it that the Haitian-French Aid Society is closing down this facility in two weeks. I'll be sent back to Paris for reassignment."

"Oh, no, what will we do for a hospital?"

"Don't worry. Lucia can tend to the simple cases, and Doctors Without Borders is only fifteen miles away. I'll try to get permission to leave you our Jeep."

"I'm not sure the school can remain open. The older boys are running off to Port-au-Prince to earn a few dollars any way they can. Some are looking for their families."

"Maybe, Gloria, you should think about going home."

"I sometimes do."

"I know Henri has stopped coming back to Jacmel most nights, and you are alone."

I ignored Nadine's last statement.

"What about the school? Chaos will return without it," I said.

"Luis can hold the school together until permanent help arrives."

"You may be right. When you go back to the tent, please send the e-mail draft of my letter to Mickey."

❧ Chapter Thirteen ❧

In the middle of that moonless night, flashes of heat lightning illuminated a starless sky. Rain pounded on the tin roof and I thought I heard occasional drops hitting the table in the next room. In my bare feet I stumbled into the kitchen, found some large cooking pots, and placed them under the holes in the roof to catch the raindrops.

I could feel the dampness of the saturated ground creep up into my body. Every muscle ached. I was exhausted, but couldn't sleep. I was scared. What if the house flooded from the saturated ground under its flimsy foundation? What if more rain poured through the leaky roof and through the windows which were perpetually open to the elements...no panes, no shades, no shutters?

Amid this gloom, someone pounded on the door. I jumped out of bed, dashed into the kitchen, and grabbed a knife out of a utility drawer. Henri had a key and would've let himself in. Grasping the handle tightly in my right hand, I looked out the open window and got my head soaked, but didn't recognize this unexpected visitor.

From the size and shape of the figure, I assumed it was a man. He wore a vinyl rain slicker and a broad-brimmed hat, but I couldn't see his face.

"Who is it?" I shouted out the window.

115

"It's me, Mickey. Let me in. It's pouring."

"Mickey?"

"Don't sound so surprised. I've been searching for you all over Port-au-Prince for a whole week."

"How did you find me?"

"Let me in before I float away in all this rain and I'll tell you."

I walked to the door still holding the knife tightly. Cautiously, I opened the door just enough so Mickey could squeeze in, raindrops streaming from his clothes onto the floor.

"Why are you here?"

"I thought I'd lost you forever when I couldn't reach you by e-mail or phone. But I'm a stubborn guy."

"I know."

"I recruited a gang of retired rednecks at my breakfast club in Biloxi to help build shelters for the homeless. I showed them your picture, and they understood why I wanted to find you. Maybe we'll build you a real schoolhouse if you insist on staying in this godforsaken country. We only have about four weeks before the rainy season sets in."

"I think it's already started."

"This is only a tease. Once it really starts, it goes on for weeks. It'll seem like forever."

"I didn't answer your e-mails because I had no cell or laptop until this week. My friend, the nurse, let me use hers. I was quite ill with malaria, and a bit out of my mind."

He looked into my face, but couldn't see how pale I'd become in the dim light.

"You look beautiful to me. I assume you've recovered."

Love is blind, I thought; but there was still plenty I wanted to know.

"I'm feeling stronger every day, but who are these guys you brought with you?"

"They're retired Mississippi gamblers, over seventy, with nothing else to do. There are six of us, including me. Roofers, plumbers, construction workers, and assorted do-it-yourselfers. I'm the engineer. I sold them a bill of goods about the loose, brown-skinned young women on this island."

"The women are beautiful."

"So are you, my first girlfriend, the one I never stopped loving. The guys fell for that romantic stuff, especially since I chartered a boat from Biloxi at my own expense. This was going to be the great adventure of their golden years."

"But how did you find me in Jacmel?"

"We docked in Port-au-Prince. The waterfront was crowded with volunteers arriving, but most were going home. They couldn't always get a plane or boat out right away, so they hung out at bars drinking rum and propositioning girls. I started asking questions of those who'd been here a while but were returning to the states, although there was still so much to do."

"Haiti still needs all the help it can get, in man-hours as well as money."

"Some of the volunteers had experienced their own heroic moment, but had to go back and take care of their own families. A few heard about a middle-aged, white, good looking teacher who followed one of her adult students to Haiti after the first days of the earthquake. It was rumored she'd set up a school for homeless children in a tent city on the shores of Jacmel's beach. The bartender gave us instructions on how to get here."

"The natives are kind that way."

117

"The bars were full of Haitian-Americans from Florida, Louisiana, and Mississippi, high on north-country rum. One tough macho-man couldn't help running his mouth. He claimed that he'd pulled three children out of the collapsed rubble of a building, and then told me about this guy named Henri, a politico, who sent for a good-looking American broad who liked black men."

I dropped the knife, hauled off, and slapped Mickey across the face.

He grabbed my wrists before either of us made an attempt to pick up the knife that had rolled under the table. He held them so tightly I knew they'd be bruised by morning, but it calmed me down.

"What do you really want, Mickey?"

"I want to build a solid schoolhouse for you, stay in this shack while building it, and love you until you beg to fly back home with me to the United States. From there we can go anywhere you want. I'm free."

He loosened his grip on my wrists and took me in his arms. I didn't resist any longer.

"Hey, Mickey, hurry," a gruff voice growled above the sound of the wind and endless rain.

"What's up? I'm not ready," Mickey yelled back.

"Are you staying or coming with us? The guy who owns that broken-down hotel in town said we could erect our tents on his property or pitch our sleeping bags in some empty rooms that are somewhat usable. There are leaks in the roof, but at least we'll be a little dry."

"Thanks, but no thanks." Mickey hollered back. "Go on ahead of me. There are tarps and netting in the Jeep, and some food and a few more bottles of rum. I'll see you tomorrow."

Against my better judgment, I let Mickey spend the night with me.

By morning, I had to admit to myself that I might be in love with two men. One was somewhere in the country making a better world for his fellow Haitians, or making babies to repopulate the region; the other was in the kitchen flipping pancakes made from tapioca flour ground from the cassava plant, then fried in coconut oil. Mickey was cavorting around the kitchen in his blue shorts and no shirt, exposing his stocky chest to whoever might come through the door. He was singing, "Once in love with Amy, always in love with Amy..." off-key as he set the rickety ice-cream-parlor table with paper towels to make the humble kitchen look like a café.

A shock of white hair kept falling in his face, but he was oblivious to it. His legs had retained their muscular shape from his days as a soccer player; his skin bore the soft, ecru complexion of a mestizo, but his features were pure Caucasian.

The knife that had fallen on the floor the night before had been picked up and put away on the magnetic cutlery bar above the sink.

He didn't hear me slip into the bathroom and brush my teeth. I came back to bed and there he was, waiting for me; the pancakes were on hold. One of the locals I'd befriended in the camp kitchen told me that cassava pancakes were delicious sprinkled with sugar, even when cold.

"Good morning, hon. It's almost noon; time to get up. I'm surprised the guys aren't hollering for me to get my ass over to the hotel."

"Do we really have to get out of bed?"

"Yea, but I'd like you to come with me, although first we can stop at the tent site or whatever you call it, and you can show me around."

"Lately we've named it the Haitian Villas, USA."

Mickey, halfway out his side of the bed, kind of smiled, and gently shoved me out the other side.

"You win," I said.

Both of us dressed quickly. I had trouble starting the Jeep; the engine was probably soaked from the night's rain. Mickey took the wheel from me. I don't know what he did, but the engine gave a frightening roar and started. I directed him toward the sea.

We didn't talk during the five-minute ride. I savored our togetherness; I think he did too. But I still had some unanswered questions about why he was suddenly obsessed with helping the Haitians. What was in it for him?

As we approached the multicolored tents, a soccer game was in progress on the beach. Luis was playing instead of teaching. Boys and girls were kicking the ball or bouncing it off their heads, but kept their hands behind their backs or up in the air. We stopped to watch as a tall girl kicked the black and white ball offside and it landed at Mickey's feet. The consummate athlete, Mickey grinned broadly, pointed his toe at the ball and kicked it to Luis who was nearing the goal posts. Luis was ready and kicked the ball with such power that it went into the net and through the goalie's hands. Nothing could stop it. Point scored; the team won 3-2.

"*Ankouraje, Aplodi, Ankouraje, Aplodi,*" the children shouted, and Luis's teammates lifted him up onto their shoulders. They carried him over to Mickey, and then put their hero down. The man and the boy shook hands.

"Good playing," Mickey said.

"Can you teach me how to kick better?"

"Yes, but first we have to get you better shoes."

The barefoot children who understood English laughed.

I smiled and waited for the excitement to calm down.

"All of you now, back to your learning centers. *Msye* Mickey has other work to do, like maybe building some houses for you."

"Ankouraje, Aplodi, Ankouraje, Aplodi," the children cheered again, oblivious to the urgency of Mickey and his fellow Mississippians' mission.

"We'll be back later," I shouted. "If your lessons are finished and it doesn't rain, maybe you can play soccer again."

☙

As we neared the *Copa Otel,* I heard the banging of hammers, the sawing of wood, and the banter of gruff male voices. Two guys were up on the roof; one was replacing missing tiles, while the other was hollering down the hole into the rooms below.

"Hey Gus, met a hot broad last night. Can you lend me some money?"

"When will you pay me back?"

"How do I know? You're the one who's working."

All the men laughed as they kept on hammering away.

"Hey, Gus, did you hear about the mayor's daughter who eloped with the cock-eyed optimist?

"No, why?"

"She wanted her gl...ass to be about half full."

"Cool it, guys," shouted Jake, the guy retiling the roof. "Here comes the boss and he's got a babe with him. Must be the one he's been drooling about all over Biloxi."

The men's voices carried, but I was sure they couldn't see me blush from that distance.

"What the fuck are you guys doing? We're here to build houses for the poor, not hotel rooms for the rich," Mickey growled at them. "Have the building supplies been delivered yet?"

Jake came down off the roof and shuffled over to Mickey in his ill-fitting work boots.

"Hi, boss. Sorry, but we owe this guy something. He gave us booze and bed last night, and wouldn't charge us. He asked if we could fix his plumbing and his roof so he could reopen his hotel. It's not a big job, and we didn't think you'd mind."

"Okay, okay, but what about the supplies?"

"We stored some of the small stuff in the broken-down utility shack behind the hotel; the rest is expected today. We contacted Sergeant Duval. He's on his way from the Port-au-Prince docks where we stored the big stuff. What an army...they work first for whoever pays first."

"Let's hope your hotelkeeper doesn't steal the nails and hammers before the bigger stuff arrives."

I admired the way Mickey handled his men. He was authoritative but kind. I hadn't known that about him. He'd been a respected captain of the soccer team in high school, but that was ages ago. On the other hand, I'd heard Henri laud it over his subordinates as if he were their entitled leader.

We heard the rumble of a heavy vehicle maneuvering the S-curve on the road leading up to the hotel. It was Sergeant Duval's familiar semi. We saw its cabin first, then the bulky freight carrier. The words HAITIAN ARMY were boldly printed across its khaki-colored sides.

The truck stopped and the sergeant came out of the cab. As he walked towards us, smiling, he waved a bill of lading. "Good morning, Myse Mickey, *Bon Jou,* Mis Gloria. I see you know each other."

"Good morning," Mickey replied curtly. "Do you have the goods?"

"Don't you trust me?" He shook the paper in his hand at Mickey. "Of course, it's all written down on this bill of lading." He turned to his driver. "Bernardo, tell Marcos and the others to unload the truck. Leave the reams of paper in the blue cartons in the back. We'll drop them at the school later. Okay, Mis Gloria?"

"Mesi, Sergeant, but where did you meet Mickey Green?"

"In a bar in Port-au-Prince. He's one smooth operator—when it comes to business, that is. But he's sure got a crush on you."

"Mickey's an old friend of mine from the states. He insists that he's loved me since I was fifteen. Can you believe that?"

"Wi, I guess, but be careful, Mis Gloria."

"Msye Mickey," said the sergeant, "be good to her. She wonderful woman. Love and teach our children. No heartbreak or rough stuff or..." And he touched his hand to the gun in his holster.

"I got ya. Don't worry, I'll treat her right. Now let's make sure you delivered all the equipment. Some will be stored here. My guy will take the boxes needed to finish this job now. The other equipment will be taken down to the school. We'll start building there tomorrow."

Mickey and the sergeant went over to the truck to watch the unloading and sign the paperwork. The truck was full of plywood, pipes, shingles, and vinyl siding, cinder blocks piled high, too. The blocks would be used to keep the prefab houses above ground level and hopefully avoid flooding. Boxes of nails, caulking, and molding were marked as well. Mickey checked off everything they'd brought from Mississippi against his duplicate bill of lading. Jake joined them, took the materials needed to repair the hotel, and went back to work with his men.

At the same time, another car rounded the S-curve and drove up alongside the truck. It was a black limousine. The driver, in his chauffeur's black cap, opened and exited the back door for the occupants. Out stepped Henri Betencourt and a tall, white-haired dignitary who looked very familiar.

Henri appeared startled when he saw me, but regained his poise quickly. "Gloria, how are you?" He didn't wait for an answer. "I hope well. We looked for you at the school, but you'd already been and gone. I left Lucia there to help out."

"I'm not sure I need her anymore."

Henri paid no attention to my answer.

"This is Lance Carter, the head of the United Nations' Haitian Relief Commission. He was once a senator from South Carolina, and has always been a friend of the Haitians."

"My pleasure, sir," I replied to the senator. "What brings you here this morning?"

"Senator Carter heard about your tricolored tent of a school and wanted to see it—among other things. Yours is one of the most successful camps in the province. Nadine told us you'd driven over to the *otel* with a man, supposedly a builder—or is he just an opportunist?"

I ignored Henri's sarcasm and directed my reply to the senator. "I've known Mickey Green since high school. What made him volunteer and bring a crew with him to build houses that will replace the tents near the schoolhouse, I really don't know. The Haitian tragedy has brought out the best in many of us. Anyway, perhaps he wants to atone for something, or find love in this devastated land. Does it really matter?

124

"Is that the only reason he's here?" Henri snickered.

"He's promised me that, if possible, he will replace the temporary schoolhouse with a more permanent one. I can't help loving him for that. He knows how urgent it is that the houses be completed before the rains come, and he wants to please me. That's more than you want to do."

"Does he have the right permits?"

"I believe so. Ask him yourself when he finishes going over the supplies with Sergeant Duval. I didn't think the housing minister was in the habit of turning away volunteers...especially volunteers with know-how and money, these days."

The senator listened intently as Henri and I parried with words, and I wondered why I once thought this Haitian was so perfect. By that time Mickey had rejoined us. The senator shook Mickey's hand; Henri refrained from doing so.

"How exciting," the senator chimed in. "I'll be in Haiti for several days. And, I want to meet with you, Mr. Green, and talk about what you're doing and how you recruited your skilled volunteers. We need more committed men and women to come to Haiti and get this country back on its feet. Where is the truck going now?"

"To the camp."

"I'm proud of you, Mr. Green. Can I count on you to tell us about your experience at a commission hearing when you get back home?"

"Sure, it'll be my pleasure. Is Gloria invited too?"

"Of course. I've heard about Gloria, too, and I can't resist a pretty woman. She's becoming a legend to the locals. In fact, I'm going to see the camp now."

The senator smiled at me. He handed each of us his business card and said, "Call my office, or e-mail me, about how and where it is best to reach you, or I'll get that information from Henri."

Henri didn't join in the frivolity. Erect but solemn, he walked back to the limo without saying goodbye.

The UN official followed him. I noticed how dignified and handsome he was.

"See you at the camp, senator. There's a hot soccer game on tap this evening," Mickey called after him.

The minute the limo left the grounds of the hotel, Mickey put his arms around my waist and pulled me close. I wasn't embarrassed at all when my lips instinctively parted and he kissed me. The men who had been worked on repairing the hotel applauded.

But I still wanted to learn more about Senator Carter.

❧ Chapter Fourteen ❧

I returned to the SUV to get out of the scorching sun. Mickey prowled around the grounds of the Copa Otel, talking with the workmen. I watched as he filled his spiral notebook with observations, measured out plots of land with a retractable tape measure, and made several calls on his cell phone.

To my surprise, he spoke French to whomever he was calling. Then I remembered that he'd taken French in high school, and the ship he served on when he was in the Navy had been dry-docked in the French district of Guadeloupe for repairs. I never considered that Mickey might have a penchant for foreign languages.

He finally meandered over to the SUV, took a tripod and site line out of the rear storage space, and stopped by the open window before going back to the hotel.

"What're you reading, hon?"

"The money section of the English edition of the *Haiti News*. I found it on the back seat of the Land Rover. It seems every scam artist in Haiti is looking for an American front man with money. Is that really why you're in Jacmel?"

I didn't wait for his answer.

"This was once a lush resort. Now it's a dumpy, impoverished town. The people are starving. They'll do anything to get roofs over their heads and jobs. What have you been promising them?"

He bent over and kissed my neck through the open window.

"Don't be foolish. I'm an American, the son of a super salesman. I always liked helping others, but I was also looking for a fast buck and opportunity. Buy low, sell high. And Haiti's going to be a gold mine for some smart operator in a few years, especially if he has the right connections."

"What are you talking about, Mickey?"

"Take this shabby, rundown hotel, for instance. We'll fix it up; install fancy chandeliers, colorful slot machines, and video games, for starters. Jacmel is only eighteen minutes from Port-au-Prince, and for those who don't gamble, it's got a gorgeous beach and well-stacked babes for girl-watching."

"What's in it for you?"

"I like to watch a well-stacked babe myself, but—all kidding aside—millions, baby, millions. The Royal Haitian Casino was the biggest moneymaker in the country before the earthquake. Now it's reduced to dust and rubble. The gamblers are still itching for action, though."

Mickey's enthusiasm was genuine, almost contagious, but I was too angry to catch it.

"We'll make it garish, but classy. That's what the gambling crowd likes. There'll be plush, private poker rooms and Baccarat salons for the high rollers. The Copa Otel and Casino will become the Las Vegas of this side of the Caribbean. Well, more like Monte Carlo."

"So that's why you came to Haiti? Here I thought you'd become a compassionate human being, and crossed the color line despite your dislike of your granddaughter's future husband because he is black."

"Don't be ridiculous, Gloria. I still don't want Melissa to marry that common Alabaman. Collard greens and ham hocks are not the life for my granddaughter. She's a classy Atlanta debutante."

"You bigoted bastard! All along you made me believe you were looking for me, your childhood sweetheart, your long lost love. I'd just be a trophy to you."

"If I wanted a trophy on my arm, I'd have snagged a younger one. You triggered this whole idea. I kept trying to figure out how to get to you, to love you, maybe live with you and get back a slice of our wasted youth. Funny, I still want you despite Henri."

He tried to caress my neck again. This time I pushed him away.

"Don't act so high and mighty, my American princess. Who do you think my connection is here in Haiti? Your noble Henri Betencourt. His family owned the Royal Haitian Hotel. They lost a fortune because of the earthquake and are being sued by everyone who was a guest or had a relative staying there. Henri's determined to get their family fortune back any way he can; I showed him a way. He'll give me all the permits I need, despite his earlier questioning. The visit with the ex-senator was just camouflage for his real intentions."

"I don't believe you."

"Ask him yourself."

It had suddenly grown quiet around the hotel. The hammering and sawing had stopped.

Mickey looked at his watch. "It's time to get back to the camp. The guys have their own plans for the evening. Daniel Beauchamp, the owner of the hotel, arranged for some women companions and island dance music. They're starved for a little sex. And you and I are expected back for a soccer game. You don't want to disappoint your students, do you?"

"And the volunteers you brought along? Are they also croupiers and blackjack dealers?"

"Some are; others are bartenders, chefs, and just bored old men."

"So what will the natives do when this hotel and casino are finished?"

"Clean, garden, and sweep. They may be able to afford those soccer shoes for their kids after all."

"And the money…where's it all coming from?"

"I scored big in Miami the last time I was there, but you'd already left for Haiti to meet Henri. I made friends with a few silent investors—gamblers like me. I financed the transportation for the guys and myself, they paid for the building supplies that were just delivered, and we've shared the sizeable deposit for the shipping containers. Inside them are prefab sections we can assemble into small houses for those ragged families living in the dirt at your tent city. The containers are on a freighter right now, and so are the gaming tables and slot machines for the casino."

"You're full of surprises, aren't you?"

"The relief organizations can't do it. Individual donations are drying up. The balance has to come from entrepreneurs, risk takers like me—and my fellow gamblers. There are calamities all over the world, and it's not raining pennies from heaven in Haiti."

I was thunderstruck. Mickey Green and Henri Betencourt were both losers. Mickey didn't care how he won his bets, and Henri wanted the power that money bought. They were as sleazy as hedge-fund operators. I could picture the two of them smoking cigars in a club, justifying the millions they'll net from buying hotels for a few cents on the dollar, and selling land at a premium to the dedicated relief agencies building homes for the poor. They totally disregarded the needs of ordinary people. Worse, the two men I admired and thought I loved were in the midst of raping a nation.

Mickey put the tripod and site line in the back of the Rover and walked around to the driver's side. Without saying a word, we headed back in the direction of the tent city. It began to drizzle.

I started wondering what I was going to do in the next few weeks. Nadine was scheduled to return to Paris, and the US Army was preparing to evacuate the island, leaving just a skeleton staff to handle emergencies. The rainy season was almost upon us, and more than a million inhabitants were still homeless. The new hotels and gambling casinos on the drawing boards hadn't yet been rebuilt, so why would tourists flock here? I'd impulsively tied my future to a brash Haitian politician and my childhood sweetheart, who was really an aggressive, charming gambler who'd dispose of anyone who got in his way.

On the outskirts of the camp, I saw Lucia. Her swollen breasts pushed open the buttons of her shirt, and her belly was growing rounder, full of Henri's dream. She was watching a cockfight, cheering wildly for the one who crowed the loudest. Rough-looking men were pushing up alongside her. How could she ever be the first lady of Haiti?

But I'd not fit that job either, with my fair skin and inability to produce an heir. There were so many lovely, homeless children in this country. Adoption could have been a solution to Henri's dilemma, if he really loved me. But somehow we had never talked about that possibility. The child wouldn't have Betencourt blood, and Henri was bound by ancient traditions that defined his masculinity.

As soon as we reached the makeshift field, Mickey stripped off his orange silk Armani shirt and donned a yellow soccer shirt, complete with emblems. Then he put on a pair of cleats that had been in the trunk of his SUV.

"Here, Gloria, this e-mail ought to make you happy. Melissa and Wilson have broken up. I can stop being a racist now and love all your little Haitians. Wilson's mother and Judith got into a hair-pulling fight at his graduation ceremony. The wedding plans are off."

Before I could react, he pushed the e-mail into my hand and ran out to his team as they practiced. The old jock was in his glory.

The game was not scheduled to start until four o'clock. Despite the light drizzle, it looked like the whole town was celebrating even before the match began. Colorful balloons were everywhere, and a vendor on the edge of the field was selling *fri bannanns* and *kola ak sikre te*.

The opposing team wore blue shirts. All the players were laughing and flirting with the girls who wore wild orchids behind their right ears, a sign of affection. Occasionally someone kicked the ball around.

I looked around the stadium and espied Henri and Senator Carter standing on the sidelines watching the preparation for the big game. I waved and caught the Senator's eye. He waved back. Then a limo pulled up and the two men left, I presumed, for a more important agenda than the soccer game.

Mickey took charge. "Cut the crap," he barked. "Are you football players or playboys?"

The boys recognized the anger in his tone. The field grew still.

"To win the game, you *gagas* have to get the ball past the keeper and into the net. Get yourself into two teams. Jose, push the other forward with your shoulder, knock him off his legs if you have to. Eduardo, use your head to propel the ball to the cage. But remember, no hands."

"Wi, Msye Soccerman, anything you say, we do."

The girls left the field, taking seats on the grass surrounding the stadium. The game began. The ball was kicked from one side of the playing field to the other, but neither team seemed able to score. I heard it all, but didn't join the crowd. I sat in the car reading and thinking about how to keep Mickey and Henri apart.

Raoul's younger brother approached the car. "Mis Gloria, Mis Gloria, come quickly, the *foutbal*, or soccer game, as you call it, has started. The rain has stopped. Enfimye Nadine gave me this message to give you. She said to tell you it was from Senator Lance Carter."

"Thank you, Raoul the younger."

"Don't joke with me. My name is Raphael. Only one year more before they let me play in the big leagues."

I took the e-mail, tucked it into my pocket next to the one Mickey had given me, and hurried across the grass to the field. I could hear Mickey encouraging the team. Raphael ran to the storeroom to get fresh soccer balls for the second half of the game.

Alongside a bush, a few feet from the field, I heard strained sighs mingled with the cries of a woman as she retched. I drew closer.

"Help me, help me," Lucia gasped. Blood flowed from between her legs, staining her clothes and turning the ground red. I bent down and cradled her in my arms.

"Lucia, try to stay calm. We'll get you to the hospital. Nadine will be there."

"No, you must stop the bleeding. Too early. Baby not ready, Mis Gloria. Henri will be so disappointed if I lose it. They

133

smeared *mwen vajen* with the losing cock's blood. Then they laughed, crowed 'cock-a-doodle-do,' and raped me."

"Oh, my God," I gasped as I rocked the girl. She was shaking in my arms.

Halftime was almost over when Raphael came rushing by, carrying a large net full of replacement soccer balls to the game.

"Raphael, stop. Leave the balls near that ebony tree. Get to the capitol and bring Myse Betencourt even if you have to drag him out of a conference. But first get anyone left at the hospital to help me get Lucia to the emergency room. Make sure they bring clean sheets."

"What's wrong?"

"Everything. I think Lucia is losing her baby."

"Oh, no."

"Take my bicycle. Find Henri even if you have to break into the senate chambers," I screamed.

Despite this new emergency, I could hear Mickey shouting orders at his yellow-shirted team. The players shouted, "Aplodi, Mickey," honoring him each time one of them scored. He'd been a good teacher, but I'd lost any interest that I'd had in the game. All my concerns and feelings were for Lucia. It was too early for her to deliver a live baby.

There were few sick patients on cots in the hospital, only those who couldn't be moved to the stadium. Tears ran down my face. The baby was the one thing Henri wanted most, a replacement for the wife and child who'd been murdered when a band of guerrillas broke into his house one night two years ago. He was their target, but was attending a rally in the next town, so they killed those he loved. When I met him, Henri had come to America to try to forget, master the English language, and return home to bring stability back to his native Haiti. No one expected an earthquake.

I knew that someday he'd replace the murdered woman when he grew restless and met someone more exciting, but a child...that was another matter.

A few of the older girls came running toward me, carrying a large white sheet. We lifted Lucia off the ground, put her in the middle of the sheet, knotted the corners as if it were a hammock, and carried her to the hospital. In seconds she was on a scrubbed kitchen table covered with an immaculate cloth. Her legs were parted and raised up to rest on sanitized, corrugated cartons, and she was prepped for giving birth.

Nadine was already there, gloves on her hands, instruments at her side.

"Push, push, Lucia," Nadine urged.

The girls assisting her had basins of warm water ready to wash the newborn.

Lucia screamed, "No, it's too soon; it's too soon."

"We're running out of time. Push, one more time. Push."

Lucia's head fell to the side in exhaustion.

Nadine's experienced hands delivered a tiny infant. Everything was wrong. The baby boy was not breathing. He was stillborn, and his mother was dead.

Tears streaming down their faces, the older girls cleaned up the baby and Lucia before Raphael could find Henri and get him back from Port-au-Prince.

The soccer game had ended. There was no more shouting. The news of the stillbirth had somehow reached the field. The sea grew calm, its waves soundless as they reached the shore. Even the birds stopped chirping. It became a funeral instead of the fun day they'd all anticipated.

I couldn't stop crying. Mickey left both teams cooling off by swimming naked in the sea, their uniforms tossed on the beach. He didn't join them but, wet and disheveled, he'd rushed from the match to the hospital. He tried to comfort me.

My clothes were a mess, covered with blood and other birth fluids. I undressed, threw my shorts and polo into a corner of the room, and then stumbled into bed.

That night Mickey held me close, but we did not make love. It was comforting to have him in my bed, although I knew our affair was ending. Mickey belonged with Judith. She seemed a much better match for him, and certainly a more enthusiastic gambling partner. I was confident they would patch things up now that Melissa had broken up with Wilson.

I suddenly remembered Nadine stuffing an e-mail from Senator Carter into my pocket earlier in the day when I'd found Lucia bleeding on the ground. I slipped out of Mickey's arms without waking him and hoped it had not been lost in the ensuing chaos of the day. The crumpled message was still in the pocket of my shorts and I retrieved it, went into the kitchen and read it by the light of a single candle.

Dear Gloria,

I hope this message reaches you. An emergency in Washington made it necessary for me to return to the Capitol tonight. Sorry I had to miss the soccer game.

Although we have only met recently, your dedication to the children of Haiti, and your friend Mr. Green's practical approach to rebuilding the country were impressive.

The President has appointed me to head up a private investigation of the Haitian situation to see that our monetary and material contributions are not misappropriated, but used wisely. Your project in Jacmel and your testimony in Washington would be of interest to him.

I have instructed my secretary to contact you re: hotel reservations and plane tickets to Washington D.C. Testimony before the house subcommittee on Haiti is expected in three to four weeks.

We are lucky to have an organized, attractive woman with a kind heart making a difference. I've been told that you're a writer as well as a teacher. I think we might have a lot in common. When you are in Washington, we can get to know each other better and share our objectives for Haiti. It would be interesting to explore our feelings on other topics.

Please consider extending your stay in Washington.

Yours truly,

Lance Carter

I was surprised, but not displeased. Lance Carter was no Bill Clinton. He was handsome in a more refined manner. I never felt he was undressing me while we talked, although he'd obviously looked me over. The senator, I believed, knew nothing about Henri and Lucia, or Henri and myself. That was a good thing.

I put the message into my toiletry case and crept silently back into bed. Mickey didn't even stir. I stayed as far away from him as the width of the bed would allow. I would decide what to do in the morning.

Lance Carter was certainly bright and charming. Perhaps our meeting promised an interesting beginning for us both.

137

I awoke the following morning just as the sun rose. Mickey was gone and Henri must have arrived at the camp late last night, slept there, and was now busy arranging a funeral for Lucia and the baby.

I heard screams and shouts coming from the road in front of the house. Slipping on a floral muumuu, I went to the door to investigate. The sound vibrated through the hurricane-damaged sugar-cane fields that separated the north side of my tiny dwelling from the Copa Otel.

Putting on sneakers, I traversed the path between the humbled canes and came upon crowds of men gathered in front of the otel.

"Go home, *etranjes*. Foreigners go home now!"

They carried signs—some in Haitian, some in English—that read:

WE NEED JOBS

OUR FAMILIES ARE HUNGRY

THE BABY IS SICK. WHERE ARE ALL THE DOCTORS YOU PROMISED?

NEED A PLACE TO SLEEP TONIGHT

Their machetes and axes were looped through their belts, although they made no move to use them. But desperation permeated the air, and anything could happen.

Mickey was pointing a shotgun at the crowd, and his motley mates held knives and smaller arms intended to disburse the mob. Instead of firing, someone handed Mickey a megaphone. He lowered his shotgun and addressed them.

"Shut up for a minute. Look at me. I've put down my shotgun, so hold your fire. Jobs are coming. Go home to your women and children. We start excavating tomorrow for an annex to the hotel that will house our workers and their families. Meanwhile, we'll be repairing the main building and getting the casino ready for tourists. There'll be jobs for every man or woman who wants one. "

A six-foot, six-inch Haitian with a booming voice translated Mickey's words, sentence by sentence, to the crowd. Awed by his soaring presence, they grew quiet and listened.

"Why should we believe you?" someone shouted back.

"The container ship carrying prefab housing sections is due to dock on Friday morning in Port-au-Prince. Trucks are standing by to bring the cargo to Jacmel. If you don't believe me, call Henri Betencourt at the housing minister's office. He's issued the permits."

The impressive translator repeated his message in Haitian.

The response of the crowd was thunderous. Mickey was hoping they understood what was happening.

An open Army truck came into view. All the soldiers were holding rifles aimed skyward. They fired the guns into the air; it was suddenly silent. My friend Sergeant Duval, now sporting a captain's insignia on his uniform, came out of the cab.

"I come," he said, "as the representative of the government, at the request of the minister of housing. He wants to make sure that your families are not hungry."

At that cue, the soldiers began throwing out tins of k-rations.

"Take these back to your families," Captain Duval continued. "They will not be hungry tonight. Come back tomorrow at eight a.m. sharp. Msye Mickey Green is telling the truth. Henri Betencourt will be here to cut the opening ribbon for a thousand-unit housing project. Today he is attending a funeral."

Heads bowed, signs dropped, the men scrambled to pick up as many k-rations as they could carry. One by one, they appeared to be returning to wherever they'd come from earlier. They chanted as they marched:

Nou se yon pep
Nou doue viv,
Jou Eleksyion an-ap rive
Pou kimoun ki nap vote?
Henri Betencourt? Henri Betencourt?
Montre nou ou konsene
Na vi-n travay demen.

A few of the workers, raised their fingers in the gesture "V" for victory, and shouted in English:

We are the people,
We shall survive,
Election Day is coming,
Who shall we vote for?
Henri Betencourt? Henri Betencourt?
Show us that you really care
We'll be here to work tomorrow.

Mickey wasn't really a bad guy, but I didn't stop to say anything to him. I ran back to the beach hoping to see Henri one more time. I learned from Nadine that Lucia and the baby had already been buried. Although he heard the rioting at the otel, Henri returned to Port-au-Prince without even trying to appease the protestors, or even stopping to say goodbye to me. I never got to tell him how sorry I was about his latest tragedy, but maybe he knew that.

I reread the letter from Senator Lance Carter, and walked slowly up the road to the house, intending to start packing.

❧ Chapter Fifteen ☙

I entered the house through the broken screen door in the back, bypassing the kitchen, and found Mickey's sweaty soccer clothes and the shorts, T-shirt, and underwear I'd worn yesterday tossed all over the bedroom floor. A lace-trimmed lavender nightshirt, turned inside out, lay on the unmade bed. In our haste to rush out to the commotion at the Copa Otel, Mickey and I had just thrown everything on the floor. It made the house look shabbier than ever.

But sitting on a rickety chair in the center of the mess was Henri, reading some documents and checking his watch. I stood and watched him for a few minutes. He looked unhappy and impatient, but very handsome. He obviously hadn't heard me come in and, and I hadn't seen his car parked out front.

"Henri, what are you doing here?"

He turned around to face me. He looked tired and somber.

"Waiting for you, my lost cheri."

Henri was a smooth talker, but I ignored that talent this time.

"Nadine said you'd returned to Port-au-Prince."

"I couldn't go without seeing you. I've hurt so many people."

Henri sprang up, leaned against a wall, and then pounded his fists against it until specks of paint fell to the floor. I'd never seen him lose control this way before. It scared me.

"It's my fault that Lucia is dead. I should not have misled you about my intentions. My cousin Nicole, who was expected to run for reelection, is ill with cancer. The politicos thought the country needed to present a stronger image to the world; our men were becoming soft, like women. So my uncle suggested I take her place on the ticket. The Betencourt name would win it for me. But he insisted I put you aside until after the election, especially since you're a gringo. I needed at least an heir, if not a native wife."

Henri paced up and down the small room, walking around the clothes still littering the floor.

"And you thought I would sit by and work at the campsite while you roamed the country looking for votes and impregnating young girls."

"More than anything, I want to run and win the election at the end of the month—just as Obama did—to keep the office in Betencourt hands and help my people."

I wanted to charge at Henri and pound my fists against his chest, but my feet remained glued to the floor.

"So you pushed me aside for political reasons, you bastard."

Henri ignored my outburst.

"I promised my followers so much, and I've not delivered. I know it's only been a few months since the earthquake. Life has always been difficult here for the poor, and the earthquake killed 250,000 of us. A million live in leaky shacks, many are hungry, and the black market is thriving. Promises, promises. Where are the jobs? Our men have lost their self-respect. I trusted Mickey to redevelop the town of Jacmel, to make it a better place—an example for the rest of the country. I hope I'm not disappointed."

"Maybe you won't be. Mickey's a gambler, not a crook."

"I hope you're right. Let me stay here tonight, ask your forgiveness, and show you how much I love you."

I knew that if I let Henri stay, our affair would start all over again. So I swallowed hard and said, "No way. But neither can Mickey."

"I have a feeling he and I will be sharing a mattress on the floor of an unfurnished room at the Copa Otel. I need to be there tomorrow morning to cut the ribbon for the start of the housing project. A lot of voters will be there looking for jobs."

"You're right. I'll pack up Mickey's things and you can take them to him. I don't want to see either one of you back here."

"I expected your refusal, Gloria, but I had to try anyway."

I took the suitcase from the shelf of the storage bin, leaving Henri pacing around the clothes on the floor. I packed Mickey's belongings in it and topped off the contents with his muddy soccer shoes. Everything smelled damp and musty. I frantically zipped up the bag, like a crazy woman, as Henri stared at me.

"You hate me, don't you, Gloria? You blame me for Lucia's death and the death of the baby. I didn't even look to see if it was a boy or girl. Did you?"

"It was a boy. I don't blame you for his death; I blame you for the conception. Lucia was an innocent. And I was disposable. At my age, I should have known better."

"Love has nothing to do with age. Besides, this is Haiti, not Florida. Our women enjoy being sexually active before marriage, and our men relish satisfying them. Was Mickey a better lover than me? No, don't answer that question. But we could have adopted Lucia's baby when it was born and then, perhaps, married. But you were impatient."

"You never told me that, even though you knew I couldn't have children. Did you think of that just now?"

"I was busy trying to put a country together."

"And as I watched Lucia's belly get bigger and bigger, I grew angrier and angrier. She seemed to follow me everywhere. You were never here. Mickey was fun and allayed my anger, if only for the moment."

"They say a gambler is always fun."

"Not always."

"What are you going to do now?"

I sat down on the bed and tried to compose my thoughts.

"I'm going back to Florida for a while before flying to Washington in October. I've been asked to testify before a House committee investigating the use of US funds in Haiti."

"Is that why ex-Senator Carter was asking so many questions about you?"

"What did you tell him?"

"Nothing much."

There was silence for a moment. Henri fidgeted with his papers. I'd exhausted my vocabulary.

"When are you leaving?"

"For Florida? In a few days. I have some unfinished work to do at the tent city."

"Call me when you know. I'm not ready to say *orevwa*. I'd like to drive you to the airport."

Henri rose, put his files into a briefcase, and started towards the front door.

"Don't forget Mickey's suitcase."

He turned back, came to me, knelt alongside the bed, and kissed me on the cheek. I grew warm. My hands trembled as I pushed him away.

"Is there any chance you might come back, Gloria?"

"I don't know."

The loneliness and futility of being in Haiti suddenly overwhelmed me. Henri, the passion in my life, had left; Mickey, the fun in my life, was no longer welcome. Neither offered me a happy ending. I'd seen enough misery in Haiti to last me a lifetime, and I didn't enjoy being the focus of a love triangle.

I slathered my skin with insect repellent and headed for the campsite. It was drizzling more frequently these days, but the coolness of the rain revived my somnolent spirit. I knew this was only a prologue to the storms expected in the coming weeks.

Unnoticed, I entered the campsite and watched the children sitting in groups on the beach, trying to catch the sea breezes as they studied. Each cluster was led by a recently arrived volunteer from REACH OUT, a consortium of small colleges offering students a year of credit for every ten months spent abroad teaching underprivileged, sometimes illiterate, children in underdeveloped countries. Luckily, Haiti was one of the countries sanctioned as underprivileged by the UN.

"Hi Jose, hi Amelia, hi Raoul," I sang out as I headed up to the big tent in search of Nadine.

"Hi, Mis Gloria," they shouted back. "When are you coming back to teach us? We miss you."

"Soon," I answered, ashamed that I'd be leaving them in a short time.

I found Nadine in the hospital section of the tricolored tent. She was tending to a few sick patients not yet transferred to other hospitals.

"Nadine."

"Wait, I just have to distribute a few more meds."

I watched her in her immaculate light blue nurse's uniform, wearing the peaked cap favored by European hospitals. I'd never seen her lose control.

In minutes she joined me and, to my surprise, we hugged.

"When do you leave for Washington?" she asked.

We sat down together on a small leather couch in the passageway.

"Not sure. In fact, I want to e-mail Senator Carter, if you don't mind."

"You know where the computer is."

"It can wait. Tell me, why do you keep traveling around the world with a relief organization? Isn't there anyone waiting for you in Paris?"

"There's another woman living with Philippe in our apartment on the Left Bank. She's a young dancer from the Le Ballet de Paris. He wanted us both."

I started to laugh and cry at the same time.

"What is it with these middle-aged men? A need to reaffirm their youth? Are you going back to fight for him?"

"Are you going to fight for Henri? Or Mickey?"

"I don't think so."

"Me neither, although I'm Catholic and won't give him a divorce."

"I want a man who desperately wants me and no one else. I want a man who, when he sees me, wants to hold me in his arms, and when I'm not with him, yearns to come home and share my bed. Just any handsome guy won't do."

"Good luck, Gloria. Let me know when you find one. Maybe he'll have a brother. Go, e-mail Senator Carter, then freshen up. Let's have dinner together so we can talk some more."

I left the hospital area of the tent site and went to the makeshift office to use the computer. Do I call him Lance? I chose the safer salutation.

From: Globaby@eol.com
To: Lcarter@haitihelp.org

Dear Senator Carter,

I haven't heard from you since your last e-mail. When is the Congressional hearing about Haiti scheduled? I'd like to stop at my apartment in Florida and rejuvenate myself for a few days before I fly to DC. Please send an e-ticket with an open return date, to the following address:

Ms. Gloria Simon
9400 Honeybell Circle
Boynton Beach, Florida 33486

Send Mickey Green's flight confirmation and hotel reservations to:

Copa Otel
P.O. Box 124807
Jacmel, Haiti

Mickey and I are just old friends.

I'm looking forward to seeing you soon.

Fondly,

Gloria

I pressed the send button and forwarded a copy of the e-mail to Mickey.

I flew out of Haiti several days later without telling Henri when my flight was scheduled. I didn't want him to drive me to the airport. I hadn't returned any of Mickey's repeated phone messages, either.

I heard hammering and sawing coming from the Copa Otel, as well as the cacophony of men's voices—talking, laughing, singing Haitian melodies. I assumed they were building housing.

Nadine was leaving a month later. The children would miss her. A licensed doctor, paid by the Haitian Relief Commission, was coming to replace her. She would remain with him, and then would gently prepare the children for the changes in personnel.

I'd been away almost five months. When I arrived home, there was so much to do. I threw away the clothes that had become faded and worn, and threw all the rest into the washing machine to rid them of any residue from what were probably contaminated waters. Next, I made an appointment to have my hair cut and highlighted, and a facial to refresh my skin.

Then I went out to buy some food.

Months of mail was delivered the day after I returned. I scanned the letters, quickly disposing of the third-class junk, and separated unpaid bills and bank statements that hadn't been forwarded to Haiti from personal communications. There was no envelope from Washington. Perhaps Senator Carter had changed his mind, and I was no longer invited to the Congressional hearing.

I turned on my computer and deleted unimportant e-mails without opening them. Of course, I opened the one from Mickey.

From: Papmick@hmail.com
To: Globaby@eol.com

Dear Gloria:

I'm so disappointed. You left without even letting me talk to you or trying to understand my dilemma. I've been busy building the annex to the Copa Otel; our contract has a date of completion written into its financial arrangements. I made a risky but potentially profitable deal with Henri Betencourt. And, in my world, a deal's a deal.

These Haitians aren't lazy, but they've never heard of overtime or hurry up. They don't know how to use modern equipment, and it takes time to teach them the nuts and bolts. They're happy with a hammer and nails, even if it's inefficient. All they want to do is finish their day's work, go home, eat dinner, and get laid.

And Judith doesn't stop calling me on the cell. I'll probably have a several-hundred-dollar phone bill when I get back to Mississippi. What should I do about her? We've been married for over forty years. I can't just dump her. But as long as she gives me my freedom, we could be happy together when this rebuilding is finished. We already have our own children, so that's not a consideration.

After Jacmel, I've had it. I'll be coming back to the good old USA. I need a few weeks to put my affairs in order, and then I'll be ready to give you all my attention. How about attending the World Championship Soccer matches in Johannesburg, and then going on an African safari with me? Or have you had it with roughing it? Where would you like to travel? Name the place. I'm willing.

I haven't received a formal invite—or a plane ticket to Washington—for the Haitian hearing. Those guys can't make up their mind when they want it held. Everyone's stuck on his own agenda. Betencourt is so busy campaigning for the presidency across this shithole of a country that he doesn't even have time to talk to me. I hope he's got the dough to pay all these workmen, because my guys and I will only bankroll this development to a certain extent. The payroll better be delivered on Friday, or there'll be rioting and bloodshed and no completed housing.

Please rethink our relationship and write to me. I miss you.

Kisses & Love,

Mickey

I busied myself around my condo, and then relaxed on the patio facing the lake. I missed the plants that had died while I had been away; I'd left in such haste I hadn't even given them to a neighbor to care for. I wanted to block out the rotting houses, the grotesque limbless survivors, and the traumatized, homeless children at the camp, so I closed my eyes and visualized a happier tomorrow. I fell asleep for an hour, and it was dusk when I awoke—time to reconnect the lamps, the television and CD player, and the answering machine. I'd turned on the computer earlier, but stayed away from it because I didn't want to answer Mickey's message. But he was persistent. The next day, there was another e-mail from him.

From: Papmick@hmail.com
To: Globaby@eol.com

Dear Gloria:

Judy telephoned today to say that an invitation for me to appear at the hearing on October 25, 2011, arrived in Biloxi this morning.

Flirting with Disaster ~ Janet S. Kleinman

How did Senator Carter get my Biloxi address? Maybe Henri gave it to him. Though I'm sure senators, even retired ones, have their private sources. She said it was addressed to Mr. and Mrs. Mickey Green, so she opened it. Judy is so excited about my going to DC that she insists on going with me. She's shopping for a new dress right now. If I ask her to stay home, she'll blow the roof off the house; if I refuse to go, I can be held in contempt of Congress. Either way, it's a big mess. I don't know how to stop her. Any suggestions?

Help!

Kisses & Love,

Mickey

❧ *Chapter Sixteen* ❧

Although the senator's office was in the process of getting hotel reservations and e-tickets for Mickey and me, a formal invitation engraved on embossed governmental stationery arrived by special delivery at my house two days after I heard from Mickey.

CONGRESSIONAL HEARING

Before the House Appropriations Committee

Rayburn House Office Building

Independence Avenue & South Capitol Street

Subcommittee on Haitian/ US Relations

Honorable John Shays presiding

October 25, 2011, 9 a.m.

You are cordially invited to testify at this hearing to share with this committee the findings of the Haitian Relief Commission established by the president of the United States under the direction of the Hon. Senator Lance Carter, Ret. The goal of the committee is to determine the humanitarian and economic impact of the millions of dollars, materials, and volunteers pledged and provided to rebuild Haiti since the January 2010 earthquake.

Please return the enclosed response card by August 25, 2011. Hotel reservations will be made for you as soon as your RSVP is received. Flight confirmations to follow.

Senator Lance Carter, Ret.
U.S. Representative
UN Haitian Relief Commission

There was a handwritten postscript on the bottom:

P.S. I will be in touch next week concerning other matters. Sincerely, Lance Carter

I was honored and excited to be included in this governmental hearing. Without hesitation, I checked "yes" on the response card, sealed the stamped return envelope, and dropped it into the mailbox. I was proud that my work at the tent city in Jacmel had been recognized as an important example of what could be done to rescue Haitian youngsters from continued illiteracy and the emotional distress caused by the earthquake.

The days flew by, filled with activities both social and sporting. I also resumed teaching English to newly arrived immigrants. I edited my journal and read everything I could find about Haiti. I had no idea what kind of questions the committee members would ask.

One morning as I was eating breakfast and reading the newspaper, the phone rang.

"Good Morning."

"Ms. Gloria Simon?"

"Yes."

"I'm Joanne Morgan, an aide to Senator Lance Carter. We received your RSVP and we're glad you will be able to attend the hearing on October 25. Senator Carter asked me to call and advise you that reservations will be made for you at the Mayflower Hotel for your arrival on Tuesday, October 24, the day before the hearing. Your checkout will be determined upon arrival. Is that all right with you?"

"It sounds fine. I hear it's quite an elegant hotel. Is it within walking distance of the Capitol?"

"It's just a few blocks away. If the weather is inclement, there's limousine service at the hotel to bring you to the Rayburn Building. There's also a spa and fitness center for your enjoyment. The senator hopes you'll like it. He generally stays there when he's in Washington."

"Are the other participants in the hearing staying there too?"

"Some are; others aren't. There are so many good hotels in Washington. Not everyone is worth five stars."

I gulped at that statement and was glad I wasn't in the midst of chewing.

Suddenly, her tone changed. "By the way, Ms. Simon, the senator was hoping you could stay on a few days after the hearing ends."

I sensed a coldness in Ms. Morgan's voice, but I ignored it.

"We still have some unfinished business to take care of. Is something the matter?"

"Of course not. We're both professionals."

"Then you can tell Senator Carter that it might be possible for me to stay two or three more days? I haven't visited the capital for a few years. I'd like to spend some time at the Smithsonian and visit Arlington Cemetery. I have a nephew buried there. Thanks so much for calling."

We both hung up at the same time.

I wasn't too pleased about Ms. Morgan's coldness coming through loud and clear when we talked about my staying in DC a few more days. I didn't dare ask if Mr. and Mrs. Mickey Green were staying at the Mayflower too. And I had no idea if Henri Betencourt had been summoned to the hearing.

I hadn't heard from him, and though I knew that was for the best, I wanted to know what was really going on in Haiti. The Florida and New York newspapers made an occasional fuss about the chaos still surrounding the rebuilding, but their reporters were too busy covering the upcoming primaries and projected midterm House and Senate elections. They didn't seem to care about the political turmoil on that forsaken island.

I dialed Pierre Betencourt's home. Before I could hang up, a female voice answered, *"Alo."*

"Is Dr. Betencourt at home? This is a friend of his brother Henri."

"Lakay peson."

I hung up without leaving a message. If Pierre wanted to talk with me, he could call back using caller ID.

Did I really want to get involved with the Betencourt family again?

I arrived in Washington the afternoon before the hearing. The hotel was magnificent. Originally built in 1816, and continuously expanded and remodeled to rival the grand palaces of Europe, it now had the modern amenities of Internet, flat screen televisions, and movies on demand. My room had a huge canopied bed with floral damask coverings. It faced the National Mall, bordered by the Lincoln Memorial on the east and the Capitol Building on the west.

I unpacked, exercised in the new fitness center, and then went for a swim. Adjacent to the women's lockers was a beauty salon. I stopped in to have my hair blown out and a manicure; it was important to my ego that I look good tomorrow. It was a public hearing, and although I expected Mickey to be there, maybe Henri Betencourt would be, too.

I walked into the lobby and ordered an apple martini at the bar, but saw no one who even looked Haitian. Rather than eat dinner at a table for one, I ordered my meal sent to my room. Then I reread my journal, highlighting items that might be relevant and refreshing my memory about life in Haiti. But the images of horror, destruction, and death were imprinted on my soul; I didn't need to be reminded of them. Instead, I smiled to myself as I visualized groups of children—some happy ones—studying English at the edge of the sea.

I watched the old classic, *Some Like It Hot*, laughing at the antics of Marilyn Monroe, Tony Curtis, and Jack Lemmon, and then went to bed. I needed to be well rested for tomorrow.

I walked down Independence Avenue toward the Capitol, enjoying a beautiful early fall day. Although the leaves were still green, the air was crisp. I entered the building, showed my invitation, and went through security. An usher directed me to the Rayburn Building, Room 1216.

The hearing room had polished leather chairs on the dais, where Representatives John Shays, Thomas Foreman, and Margaret Owens sat, watching the invitees enter. John Shays was identified as committee chairman.

Lance Carter sat in the first row of seats facing them. A page escorted me down the dividing aisle and seated me directly behind him. Other men and women filled the row, and then I saw them—Mickey and his wife, sitting two rows behind me. Mickey, looking serious but uneasy, was wearing the pinstriped Armani suit I remembered from happier days. Judith's bleached-blonde hair clashed with her purple designer suit. Her eyelashes were a nightmare of mascara, and she seemed jittery. A large diamond sparkled on the fourth finger of her right hand. She was expensively dressed, but lacked good taste.

First we all stood for the salute to the flag and the Pledge of Allegiance. Then John Shays banged his gavel and started the proceedings. After introducing himself, he introduced Foreman and Owens. All were members of the House Appropriations Committee.

"Thank you all for coming here today. This hearing will help us recommend whether to expedite and extend the aid package we pledged to help Haiti recover from the devastation wrought by the January earthquake. To that end, we have invited retired Senator Lance Carter, the chair of the UN Committee on Haitian Affairs, to address us and to introduce those of you who have participated and continue to participate in the rebuilding effort."

I didn't realize how handsome Senator Carter was until he got up to speak. His nose was straight; his blue eyes had flecks of gold and shone through his rimless glasses. A head of well-groomed white hair reminded me of our charismatic former president, who was now the UN special envoy to Haiti. Senator Carter was tall and slim, and looked like he exercised regularly. Somewhere I'd read that he liked to play golf.

"Good morning. I have recently returned from a twenty-three day trip to Haiti to assess the damage on the island and prioritize the resources needed to rehabilitate it. Over 250,000 Haitians, as you know, died as a result of the earthquake, and over a million are still homeless. Through the kindness of relief organizations, individuals, and the generosity of various countries, though many have neglected to honor their pledge, hunger and disease are under control. Volunteer medical groups have managed to prevent outbreaks of malaria and typhoid. Orthopedists in tent hospitals have fitted artificial limbs to those unfortunates whose arms or legs were crushed under the rubble of fallen buildings. But my heart still hurts when I see those who haven't been reached by the largesse of volunteers and foreigners.

"Education is reemerging in tents and patched-up school buildings. But lack of shelter remains the most perilous enemy of the recovery. Relief organizations and private contractors have employed creative solutions to these problems, but that is limited to small areas. I tremble to think what will happen when the heavy rains descend on the island.

"We have invited the innovators of several model projects to describe what they accomplished with little governmental help. My committee trusts that what you hear today will be an incentive to expand distribution of materials and monetary aid so these projects can be replicated throughout Haiti. This is the country's only hope."

The first speaker was a physician from Doctors Without Borders, followed by a water purification specialist, an agriculturist, an infrastructure expert, and an airport designer. Each expert handed a detailed written summary to the recording secretary.

Mickey Green was the next speaker. He squeezed past his wife and came to the front of the room. Stumbling over his words, he stuttered for a moment, then gained control of himself and the microphone.

I turned to look at Judith. She sat tight-lipped and angry.

"I went to Haiti," Mickey began, "as an independent contractor with a group of comfortable and bored, but skilled, men. Sitting at a bar in Biloxi, Mississippi, we knew we wanted to do something that would make a difference. We rented a boat to get to

158

Haiti and, once there, found a site and imported prefabricated, do-it-yourself sections. The inhabitants of Jacmel, a small resort town south of Port-au-Prince, assembled the sections into small houses."

He never mentioned the real reason he had come to Haiti. I knew that, but it was none of the panel's business. The representatives listened attentively, and took notes.

"Excuse me," Rep. Forman interrupted. "We hear that you have reopened a gambling casino in the old Copa Otel. Is that correct?"

"It sure is. There are still lots of Haitians with money. Not in Jacmel, but those who have it will travel to gamble if we make it attractive enough. Not all the players want to bet on a cock fight."

There were snickers throughout the room; Chairman Shays banged his gavel.

Mickey continued, "The money earned from the gamblers is used to pay the Haitians who are building the houses behind the hotel. Their families will move in first, but we can only build a limited number. The Haitian government, through the influence of the Housing Minister, Henri Betencourt, was helpful, but they have no money to expand the program. They're waiting for money pledged by other countries of the world, and that's slow in coming. My guys are tired and would like to turn the project over to a government authority, but we'll keep control of the casino. We've promised to donate half the profits to the building of houses for the homeless and we will, but we're volunteers and it's time for us to go home to our families."

"How much money would you need to expand your program to other towns?"

"Several million; less if the government allows the expansion of gambling."

"I'm not a fan of gambling," Rep. Owens commented.

I wondered why the committee was so interested in Mickey's gambling activities. Weren't there other business opportunities that interested them in Haiti? At that point Mickey caught my eye. He'd obviously seen me come in. We smiled faintly at each other.

"Thank you, Mr. Green. Keep us informed on the progress of your housing project, or any other businesses you choose to engage in. This committee is planning to visit Haiti and your model town soon. You may return to your seat."

Mickey walked up the aisle and gave me a broad smile as he passed the second row. Since I was sitting behind Senator Carter, he didn't see it. Then Mickey sat down next to his wife. They didn't even look at each other.

"Is Henri Betencourt, housing minister of Haiti, in the room?" queried Chairman Shays.

There was no answer.

Chairman Shays repeated the question. No response.

"I guess not," concluded Rep. Foreman.

So, Henri had been invited but chose not to come. It was my turn.

"Good morning, ladies and gentlemen. I'm Gloria Simon, a retired teacher and writer from Florida who's tutored many Haitians in English. When the earthquake shook the country, some of my students disappeared, taking off for Haiti in any kind of transportation they could find. Their families and friends were there. It was the country of their birth. A Haitian-American leader I knew stated they needed services for the children who were wandering aimlessly around the country. There were few teachers and many destroyed schoolhouses. I decided I had the time to make a difference and flew to Haiti."

"On a commercial airliner?"

"No, on a private plane."

"What did you do when you got there?"

"I made contact with a member of the government, who put me in touch with Nadine Cheval, the head nurse of the French Haitian mission. Coincidently, I'd met her on the plane to Haiti. She'd started a hospital campsite for the homeless and injured children wandering the streets of Jacmel, a small town ten miles south of Port-au-Prince.

"A friend who owned a Jeep got me to this earthquake-flattened town, a beautiful place at the edge of the Caribbean. In her makeshift facilities, Nadine was caring for the injured. She liked my idea of adding a tent annex to the hospital that would serve as a school for its patients, many of whom were sleeping on the beach anyway.

"My government contact made arrangements for tents to be delivered. In the meantime, with the help of the older boys who knew some English, we organized the children into groups. I taught the boys how to teach language and reading from experience charts. For recreation, with the help of Mr. Green, we organized soccer teams, and encouraged swimming.

"The Haitian Army cooperated with us. Every time they brought medicines, bandaging, and appliances to the hospital, they managed to include paper, pencils, and colored chalk—and even blackboards—from the abandoned, crumbling schoolhouses in Port-au-Prince.

"When the tents arrived, the soldiers built temporary shelters for us with the help of our older boys. One tricolored triple-sized tent served as the main building of our schoolhouse. We continued using the beach, as the weather was warm and dry. The rainy season hadn't arrived yet.

"Recently, stateside volunteers with some teacher training and some very bright college students joined us. Our children were very happy, except those who were so traumatized that nothing seemed to help."

"Excuse me," said Rep. Owens. "Do you think your model can be duplicated in other towns?"

"Perhaps in the smaller towns. Port-au-Prince must be cleaned up first. There is rubble everywhere."

"Is empathy the only reason you offered your services?"

"I knew the Haitians were quick learners from my contact with them in Florida. I'm an optimist. Once in the country, I grew to admire the people for their strength in the face of death and destruction. I wanted to help turn chaos into order, especially for the children."

"Any other reason?" queried Chairman Shays.

"I had been urged to come by a gentleman I had grown fond of."

"Is he here, Ms. Simon?"

"I do not see him."

"One final question. Would you say that US money is being used wisely to rehabilitate and save the children?"

"In some parts of Haiti, yes."

"Are you planning to return to Haiti, Ms. Simon?"

"Not permanently. It is time for the Haitians themselves to take over the tent cities and their schools…"

"Go on Ms. Simon."

"But they'll need help from tutors, like the volunteers from REACH OUT. It's a society founded by a group of Midwestern professors, specialists in promoting literacy. They had no trouble recruiting student volunteers because of the recession and a successful campus-to-campus PR campaign. It's imperative that a training school for local teachers be started immediately in anticipation of students returning to Haiti with their families in the near future."

I took a drink of water from the glass on the small table at my side. Senator Carter was smiling at me. I assumed he was pleased with my testimony. My eyes scanned the rows in front of me. Mickey and Judith were no longer there, but a pair of purple leather gloves had been left behind.

"Thank you, Ms. Simon," said Chairman Shays. I stepped down from the witness chair.

The chairman thanked Senator Carter and the other witnesses, and asked for permission to include our statements in the record. There were no nays.

"Senator," said Chairman Shays, "will you summarize the desirable goals of the Haitian Relief Commission for this subcommittee?"

Senator Carter spoke slowly, but passionately. "The aim of this group is to produce an infrastructure for the country that enables housing, jobs, and education to spread to every citizen of Haiti who so desires it. We have made tremendous progress in providing sustenance to the hungry masses and avoided unhealthy epidemics. But that's not enough. Jacmel is a beginning, and all those connected with that community deserve our thanks. A regulatory system, however, needs to be put in place to assure that political factions don't misappropriate funds collected for reconstruction.

"One more thing. It has come to my attention that modernization of the port is essential. My contacts in Port-au-Prince tell me that repairing its docks has become a political issue. So have bribes. Do you have any further questions for us?"

"No, but thank you all for coming. You have been a most cooperative group. I think we may need more facts before we increase appropriations to Haiti. For now, this session is adjourned."

Although most of the attendees had left, Lance Carter remained behind to talk with Representative Shays and his colleagues. I hesitated, sorting my papers until I couldn't delay leaving any longer, then picked up my belongings and headed out of the hearing room.

I wondered why I'd consented to stay on. Perhaps I should return to Florida the next morning, after visiting Arlington Cemetery to pay my respects to my nephew who'd been killed in the first Gulf War. We'd been such good friends as children.

Mickey and Judith were nowhere in sight. They were probably already on the way to Mississippi. Henri Betencourt hadn't been invited or had declined to come to the hearing, and I had misinterpreted Lance Carter's e-mail flirtation.

Back at the hotel, there was a hand-delivered message from Henri's brother waiting for me.

Dear Gloria:

I knew you were back in Florida, but when I phoned you I reached only your answering machine.

Now that Michelle has dropped out of the running because of ill health, Henri is so busy campaigning for the presidency in Haiti that he has no time for anything else. He did, however, know where to find you and asked me to see if you needed anything. I promised him that I'd make sure you were okay.

He was invited to Washington too, but thought it would be a conflict of interest and bad politics if he attended the hearing. He rushed me his invitation and I blended in with the others in the hearing room. There was no fuss about my first name. I found a seat way in the back so I could leave inconspicuously. Henri would've appreciated what you said— and didn't say—at the hearing. You can't contact him directly, though, because there are threats against his life and his opponents shadow him wherever he goes.

I will relay a record of your testimony to him.

Torrential rains have now started in Haiti. Cardboard houses are breaking up, floating downhill, and blocking the sewers. Cholera has started to spread from the towns to the cities, and we do not have enough medicine to control what looks like an epidemic. The homeless continue to line the streets of Port-au-Prince. I'm afraid for my brother.

Fondly,

Pierre

There I was, involved with the Betencourts again. It was my fault. I should never have contacted Pierre when I got back to Florida.

Suddenly there was a knock on the door.

"Who is it?"

"Room service."

"I haven't ordered anything."

"But someone has for you, Ms. Simon."

I unbolted the chain and peeked out into the hallway. There was a teacart holding small sandwiches and what looked like a bottle of champagne in an ice bucket. Two champagne flutes and lavender linen napkins lay alongside the bucket.

I opened the door, and the bellhop brought in the cart. As I went to my purse to get a tip, the server stopped me.

"No, madam," he said, in a clipped British accent. "It has already been taken care of. I was instructed to give you this letter personally."

Champagne for two. What to do? Drink alone? Wait? There was only one person who could have sent it. Before I could even open the envelope and take out the monogrammed stationary with Senator Lance Carter's name followed by Ret., someone rapped on the side door of my room, which connected to an adjoining room. My bedroom had once been part of a suite.

"Gloria, it's Lance Carter. Your room is adjacent to mine; it's part of the original Carter Suite. The door can be left open or locked. If you unbolt your door, I can use my key to get into your room—with your permission, of course. Washington is a hothouse of gossip. Since I'd rather none of the other guests saw us, I'd like to come in through the connecting door."

I hesitated a moment, then unbolted my side of the door.

"Why not, Lance? Shall I pour the champagne or would you rather do it? This is almost like Shakespeare's *Pyramus and Thisbe*."

I heard the senator laugh and then unlock the door and enter my room.

He came towards me and then stopped short.

"I want you to know, Gloria, that I'm a southern gentleman from South Carolina – not a woman chaser – a former senator and now a professor of Latin American Studies at the University of South Carolina.

"I also want you to know I've been a widower for eight years. That's a long time to be alone. Lucy, my late wife, was the founder of the Haitian Christian Mission. We had no children of our own and raised two of the orphaned boys, brothers we adopted through our work with the mission. Today, one is a doctor; the other a poet. I'd like you to meet them some day."

"I'd love to,"

Then he took me in his arms, and we kissed.

"I've wanted to do this from the first time I saw you in Haiti."

We forgot about the champagne.

The following morning, Lance and I prepared to visit Arlington Cemetery. He returned to his rooms, and we relocked the door separating my room from his. I could hear him showering, and he probably heard me. I hoped he'd enjoyed the night as much as I had. He had strength mingled with tenderness that I'd not experienced with Mickey or Henri. Suddenly, I wasn't in a hurry to get back to Florida.

His government limo was picking us up at nine-thirty a.m., and he'd arranged for the driver to have croissants and coffee for us so we could breakfast as we traveled. Lance had a luncheon meeting at the Capitol at noon, and I planned to go on to the Smithsonian.

A few minutes before 9:30, he knocked on the front door. "Are you ready, Gloria?"

"Coming."

This time he was waiting in the hallway, and we walked to the elevator together.

"Good morning, Senator Carter," said a conservatively dressed older man I recognized from the hearing.

"Do you remember Gloria Simon, Congressman Foreman? She testified at yesterday's hearing."

"It's my pleasure to meet you again. What you said was very informative."

"Thanks for the compliment," I replied, and then gave him my best smile.

"Lance, after the hearing, we polished off a few at the Atrium Bar. Too bad you couldn't join us."

"Next time, perhaps," Lance said. "I had other commitments."

☙

The chauffeur opened the doors of the black limo and we slid in. The vehicle headed for Arlington Cemetery while we ate our mini-breakfast.

"Whose gravesite are you going to visit?" I asked.

"My brother's. He was killed in a battle on the Yalu River during the Korean War. I haven't said a prayer for him in a long time."

We stopped at the entrance to the cemetery, where the driver showed the guards the senator's identification papers. Once through the gate, he dropped us off at the visitor's center so we could get the gravesite locations for Major Stewart Carter and Corporal Jerome Heller, my nephew. One had died for his country at twenty-eight in Korea, the other at twenty-one during the first Gulf War. Coincidentally their headstones, though erected years apart, were near each other.

We stopped to see "The Price of Freedom," Greg Wyatt's recently installed in-the-round bronze statue. It features an angel with huge wings gently holding the body of a dying unknown serviceman, protected by seven symbolic World War II heroes. The base of the statue represents the world, and is decorated with wreaths, shields, insignias, and a pair of winged eagles.

I shed a few tears and moved closer to Lance. He put his arm around my shoulders and drew me close to comfort me.

I shared my thoughts with him, "I pray the day will come when we no longer have to bury any more young heroes at Arlington Cemetery. Old soldiers will always have a home here, and be honored by us forever."

Lance said nothing, but a single tear rolled down his weathered face. Like his brother, he'd been in the service, but years later during the Vietnam War.

"Shalom and amen," I whispered as we boarded the bus that took us to the designated gravesites. White markers were everywhere, thousands of them; simple tributes to the heroes and heroines who had died for their country.

An unrelenting chill ran through my body on that sunny October morning. It was almost as if an omen had engulfed us. I had friends who worried every day about their children in Iraq. In the turmoil of our confused and violent world, another proud, unsuspecting serviceman might die for his country today.

☞ *Chapter Seventeen* ☜

While Lance scurried from appointment to appointment at various government departments, I spent time at the Smithsonian. The Air and Space Museum had always been one of my favorites, but today I lingered in the Sackler Gallery of Asian Art. I'd been collecting Japanese Imari porcelain since I was a young woman, and hoped to find a few great pieces on display at the Sackler.

That evening, I met Lance for cocktails at a private party in the courtyard of The Organization of American States, formerly known as the Pan American Union. Lush foliage surrounded the courtyard and reminded me of how Haiti must have looked before the earthquake. The reflecting pool conjured up images of the crystal clear Caribbean.

Groups of diplomats from Latin American countries stood drinking cocktails and enjoying miniature tacos. English, French, Spanish, and Creole resonated all over the courtyard. Some of the conversations were about Haiti, and I heard Henri's name mentioned a few times. Although he had many opponents in the upcoming election, one ex-premier of that country considered him the favorite to become the next president of Haiti.

Lance joined these conversations when they were in French, a language he'd studied and that educated Haitians spoke and understood. I smiled at these well-dressed men and women and listened attentively when the conversation concerned Haiti.

"The election is only four weeks away."

"He's campaigning hard and fast."

"The peasants adore him."

"So do the ladies."

"Is he married? Does he have a family?"

"I heard he's a widower. No children. But it's rumored that he recently had a white girlfriend."

"Excuse me," I interjected. "I have to go to the ladies' room."

❧

The following evening we had dinner and attended a concert at Kennedy Center. Then, in what was becoming a ritual, a limo picked us up.

On the ride back to the hotel, Lance finally asked the question I was dreading.

"Gloria, tell me honestly, what is the relationship between you and Mickey Green? I see that he has a wife."

"We are just old friends. He was my first boyfriend back in high school."

Lance didn't ask any further questions. Back at the hotel, he opened the adjoining doors, and we spent the night together. On other nights, we had made love; on this night we just held each other. A bond was growing between us. Tomorrow morning I would fly home.

My plane was scheduled for takeoff at five p.m. Lance's chauffeur arrived at three o'clock to take me to the airport.

"Where's the senator, John?"

"He was called away to a conference at the White House."

"Oh…"

"You don't say no to the president, Ms. Simon."

Weeks passed. The Florida newspapers carried stories of the failure of the Haitian government to provide adequate housing. There were pictures of the homeless living in tents and shacks on the median of the Rue de Rails in Port-au-Prince. Many families remained camped on the grounds of the National Palace, which listed precariously to the left. The *New York Times* carried a story about political unrest throughout the country. Rock stars and exiles were getting into the act, aspiring to be president of Haiti. Term limits prevented the current president from running again, and his plan for relocating the homeless to Fort National remained unfulfilled and unpopular. His party was facing the toughest opposition from a group calling itself *Nouvo Komansman*—New Beginnings—but there was no mention of its titular head or the name of its prospective presidential candidate.

Lance called several times and was always apologizing for being called away on a special assignment. I began to think he was the only diplomat in Washington who had a suitcase, a tux, and was free to travel.

Instead of doing the crossword puzzle while eating my breakfast on the balcony, the first thing I did these days was leaf through the paper looking for news about Haiti. This morning I slipped the *Herald* out of its plastic sleeve, glimpsed the headline, and gasped.

New President Elected in Haiti; Henri Betencourt Promises to Speed Up Reconstruction

And there was Henri, smiling at me from a picture on the front page. Another photo showed men, women, and children dancing in the streets and in the muddy roads where traffic was at a standstill. A fat, scantily dressed woman stood on the hood of a battered Buick and appeared to be shaking her body and playing a pair of multicolored maracas.

Before I could sit down and read the entire story, the phone rang. It was Pierre Betencourt.

"Gloria, how are you?"

"Fine—and you?"

"*Oke li te genyen.* Well, he has won. My brother is the new president of Haiti!"

"I know. I know. I'm holding the newspaper in my hand, and Henri looks happy. You must be very proud, and I hope all goes well for him."

"I will let you know when I'm flying down to Port-au-Prince. You deserve to be at the festivities. Of course, there'll be lots of jobs for all of us. Do you want to come along?"

I promised myself I would never get involved with the Betencourt family again, but the temptation to go to Haiti for the presidential swearing-in was overwhelming. I didn't want to appear too anxious.

"Perhaps. Keep in touch, Pierre. You've been a good friend."

❧ *Chapter Eighteen* ❧

The latest Caribbean hurricane only sideswiped Haiti, but brought mean downpours of rain to South County. It sounded like small stones were hitting the glass panels of the Florida room. I shivered, then lowered the shades, retreated to my bedroom, and got under the dry covers. What must it be like in Haiti, in the paper shacks that lined the streets of Port-au-Prince?

I tried to block out the weather and my recent conversation with Pierre by reading *The Black Englishman*, a romantic novel about a lonely English bride and a black doctor in 1920's India. The interracial liaison between passionate lovers in a dangerous environment made the story that much more personal. Was there a parable here I was missing?

Before I even met Henri, Mickey, with his endless compliments and suggestive e-mails, had restored my confidence and awakened the girl I'd been in my youth, when my sexual urges were first budding. A first love remains special, and its renewal at this time of my life was great fun. I hadn't had a sexual relationship for five years, although my husband and I had been far from celibate before his debilitating illness. Mickey belonged with Judith. She worshiped him in a way I never would.

Henri was the most exciting lover I'd ever had. Was it because he was younger than me? The passion began the moment he undressed me with his eyes, whispered *mwen adore ou dous mwen*, ran his fingers through my hair and down my neck. He'd cup each breast before gently squeezing them, and then move his hands below my waist until I almost begged him to consummate our lovemaking. He outlined my hips and stroked my abdomen until his fingers reached *"yo nan mitan janm mwen,"* the lips between my legs. By that time I was totally his and would do anything he wanted me to. He commanded the vessel, steering his rudder and arousing me beyond my wildest dreams. My body trembled. So did his. Ultimately we both found peace.

Yet I knew that Henri was wrong for me. I adored his youthful vigor, but I was not brave enough for a long-term biracial relationship—and certainly not a marriage, though he had never asked. It was, however, a part of my life I'd always treasure. Henri belonged with a Haitian woman, young and moldable. Despite his education and social background, he was still a macho Creole male in that respect.

Lance Carter was different; accomplished, proud, a patrician in a world of movers and shakers, one I'd always admired. He was handsome, well groomed, and cultured. We both cared about the world, and our conversations over dinner or drinks were deep and meaningful, even though we sometimes disagreed. He and I loved theatre, museums, and books. After spending a day together, we'd remove our shoes, occupy either end of the sofa, and read the newspapers, intent on keeping up with the world around us, until we both needed a human touch and reached out to one another. The newspapers fell to the floor, and Lance would slide over and hold me close. We'd kiss and caress until the urge to join as one overtook us and we retired to the bedroom. He was still a vital lover, and someone I saw myself growing old with.

The ringing of the phone broke my reverie, and unwillingly I returned to reality.

"Hello."

"It's your favorite senator."

"Lance, what a pleasant surprise. Where are you?"

"In an airport in Africa."

"I've missed you."

"And I've missed you, too."

"I'm on my way back to Washington."

"Is it possible for you to stop off in Florida?"

"No. I have a meeting at the State Department as soon as I land."

"I'm disappointed."

"Don't be. I'm not flying off again for a week. I'll come to Florida for a few days if I'm welcome."

"I think you know you're welcome."

"By the way, I've got an invitation in my briefcase to attend the inaugural of Henri Betencourt, the newly elected president of Haiti. I think our secretary of state wants me to attend; it makes for good relations. Would you like to come with me?"

I hesitated, regained my composure, and blurted out, "I'd be honored, Lance."

"Good. I've got to go now, the plane is boarding and I don't want to miss it. We'll talk more when I get home."

Imagine arriving in Port-au-Prince, with Senator Lance Carter, at a reception for Henri. Should I tell Pierre I was coming, but not with him? Or should it be a surprise to both Henri and Pierre? Perhaps I could just fade into the mass of celebrants and no one would notice I was there. Meanwhile, neither man had told me when we were flying to Haiti.

I was excited, but scared.

Lance Carter flew to Hong Kong, Jakarta, Istanbul, and Tel Aviv, but he never made it to Florida. There was always a new emergency.

"I'm sorry," he said every time he called. "I have to cancel my visit."

"I know," I'd reply. "The president comes first."

Finally, Lance set a date for our rendezvous. It would take place a day before Henri's inauguration and would be in Haiti rather than Florida. I was to meet Lance in a section of the Miami Airport reserved for government planes. Special papers would be issued so I'd be escorted to the jet once I passed inspection. My bag would be picked up at my condo and loaded on an assigned plane a day before departure.

❧

I was checking my e-mail before putting a temporary "don't send messages until…" on my computer when I spotted a message from Pierre Betencourt. Henri, unwilling to disclose his Haitian e-mail address, had written to me via his brother.

Hi, my sweet, he wrote. *Are you coming to Haiti for my inaugural?*

I digested the message with pleasure, but saw no need to reply. I was flying down anyway.

Out of politeness, I telephoned Pierre. He picked up after the third ring.

"*Alo.*"

"Pierre, it's Gloria."

"So good to hear from you. Right now I'm at my desk making arrangements for our trip to Port-au-Prince."

"That's why I called," I interrupted before he could say anything else. "I won't be going with you."

177

"Why not? Have I insulted you in any way?"

"No."

"Are you ill? Is something else wrong?"

"No, Pierre, no. I'm going to Haiti for the inauguration, but with someone else."

"Who? Anyone I know? Anyone Henri knows?"

"Senator Lance Carter. They've met."

"I don't think my brother will like that."

"I've already said yes to the senator."

"Sure you won't change your mind?"

"No, Pierre. I'll always love Henri, but I need a different kind of life. I need a different kind of man."

"You're shortchanging yourself. He's the best."

"I'll take my chances on the senator. See you in Port-au-Prince."

"*Bon chans*. Good luck, Gloria."

The credentials for my flight to Haiti were very official looking with their government seals that guaranteed there'd be no problems at the airport. I put them with my passport.

A separate envelope followed. It contained reservations at Villa Teresa in Petionville, a ten-minute ride from the National Palace. My student, a cousin of Henri's, told me that the recently repaired apartments at the capitol had been reserved for the incoming president and his family.

I'd visited Petionville when I was in Haiti. It's a beautiful suburb in the hills north of Port-au-Prince with many trees, broad boulevards and large villas, private homes, and converted inns. The wealthy owners had already repaired the residences and hotels damaged in the quake. Through its ambassador, the US government requisitioned an entire villa with suites, a housekeeping staff, and a cook. The gardens were lush, with bougainvilleas encircling a swimming pool and a tennis court.

It was hard to believe that minutes away, in the unsavory camps lining the unlit streets of the capital, young girls and old women were often savagely raped by escaped prisoners and even by their own relatives. The Haitian police did nothing. Women's groups from Florida, with the help of law enforcement volunteers, had recently airlifted tons of whistles and flashlights for distribution to the women in these lawless sites. At least it gave them a way to call for help.

My cell phone rang. I rummaged through my bag and found it before the caller hung up.

He sounded breathless and, as usual, in a hurry.

"Gloria, did you get the special delivery package I sent you?"

"Yes, Lance, but it's been days since I heard from you. Are you okay?"

"Fine, too busy to write, but not too busy to think about you."

"That's encouraging. I'm reading the papers now. Why all the specifics about the villa? Won't you be on the plane with me?"

"Maybe, maybe not. But I promise I'll be there on the first of February. The others on the plane will also be staying at the villa, but not in the same wing as you and me. It's quite a beautiful place in a safe neighborhood."

"You're an old devil." I could hear him laugh as I pondered what else to say, and then blurted out, "I can't wait to see you."

"In a few days, honey."

179

❧

Still holding the reservations in my hand, I turned on the radio. A hostess on "Haitian News Today," a program from Port-au-Prince, was interviewing Eldridge Bayou, the Haitian hip-hop singer. He was the idol of that country and its ex-pats. He composed *"Chante pou la Mizerab"* ("Sing for the Poor") days after the earthquake, and continued to give concerts all over the world to raise money for the hungry and homeless in Haiti.

Eldridge claimed to have been born in Haiti, but has no birth certificate to prove it. He says his parents brought him to the United States and raised him in Louisiana. His Petionville villa is a showplace, and he's lived in Haiti for the past five years when not on tour. As a landowner and resident, he's qualified to run as a presidential candidate in the recent election. He speaks poor Creole, no French, and bayou-style English, but the Haitians adore him, his songs, and his generosity.

After a lot of paparazzi-type questions, the hostess asked, "Since you are such a favorite with the people, why do you think you lost this election to Henri Betencourt?"

"Henri Betencourt, the proclaimed victor, used his wealth to enlist a dozen potential candidates besides himself, confusing the voters. These are simple people, and the long list of candidates split the opposition. There were also threats on my life, my family's lives, and the livelihood of my supporters."

"That's quite a charge, Eldridge."

"I love my people more than any of the other candidates, but that is not enough. In Haiti, money talks. Everyone knows that the Betencourts are the most powerful and richest family in the country. In fact, they own this radio station. A dollar for a vote can buy a meal for a family, and Henri has the most dollars. No one can even approximate how much money…"

The radio transmission from Haiti went dead.

It was hard for me to believe that Eldridge's charges about Henri were true.

❧ Chapter Nineteen ❧

To my surprise, Lance was already on the plane when I boarded. He and three other passengers were in a heated conversation.

It was a deluxe first-class jet, luxuriously appointed in marbleized leather with six seats in the forward half of the plane, and a bar separating the six seats in the tail section. I stood there, quietly waiting for him to turn and realize I had boarded.

Lance finally noticed, smiled, and welcomed me with a hug.

"Good to see you, darling," he whispered softly as he came forward and stroked my hair. He waved away the uniformed steward who'd ushered me onto the plane, and led me to a seat in the rear.

"There's more privacy here, although it's only a short flight. The agriculturists and I were having a discussion on the neglected soil of Haiti. The other passenger is that country's ambassador to the United States. We're giving him a ride home."

"How diplomatic of you."

"Drinks in twenty minutes. I'll introduce you to the others. Do you need anything, Gloria?"

"I'm fine. It gives me enough time to comb my hair and freshen up."

"You look great to me."

I gave him my warmest smile and dropped my tote bag on the empty seat next to mine. He caressed my shoulders, and then went back to the others.

Eyes closed, imagination soaring, I envisioned Lance stretched out on a king-sized bed, turning towards me, holding my head in his hands, kissing my eyelids and my cheeks. Then he licked my lips until my mouth opened and his tongue entered. I began to spread my legs.

❧

After a smooth takeoff, I unfastened my seat belt and headed to the bar. The steward had mixed up a batch of rum and mango juice cocktails. Lance introduced me to Donna and Uberto Castro—no relation to Fidel. Born in Cap Haiten, the husband-and-wife team had both graduated from Cornell University's College of Agriculture. We chatted about the possibility of growing more cacao and commercial-quality mangoes for export.

"If the Israelis could make the desert bloom," Lance interjected, "why can't the Haitian farmers add enough nutrients to revitalize their barren land? Haiti certainly has enough water."

It was a pleasure listening to Lance's rational input. He was bright, articulate, and convincing. His knowledge of the world excited me. But I tired of the technical side of agriculture and changed the topic to a more human issue—the status of women.

"I hear that there are young girls working on those farms who've been sold or just given to the landowners by their families. They're less than cheap labor—they're slaves. They're working in the fields, just waiting to be sexually abused."

The agriculturists blushed.

"That's not our expertise," said Uberto.

"Are you a feminist?" asked Donna.

183

"Why? Does it matter?" I said. "We're talking about human rights. Do you think the new president will do anything about this atrocity?"

"It's not a priority," Uberto said.

"Not a priority!" I shouted. "Slavery is over. Didn't anyone tell your government?"

The Haitian ambassador said nothing. He just continued drinking.

"Calm down, everybody," said Lance, closing the argument before it turned hostile.

"Gloria, I'll try to get you an interview with the new president. If that fails, I'll surely get you a meeting with the department of social service. There are so many Haitian women living in Florida, you might be able to organize them to help their sisters on the island. My committee will help as much as possible."

I gulped. If Lance knew about my relationship with Henri Betencourt, what would he think? I didn't know. Perhaps it would be best if he never found out.

"Gloria, Donna, Carlos, Mr. Ambassador…how about we all go back to our seats and take a rest before landing? It's only an hour until we reach Haiti."

Lance took my hand, and we walked up the aisle to our seats. He sat down in the seat adjoining mine and raised the armrest so our bodies touched. The agriculturists and the Haitian ambassador remained in the front of the plane.

Our arrival at Port-au-Prince International Airport was uneventful. We gathered our belongings, thanked the pilots, and were escorted by the steward to a waiting government limousine.

Lance sat up front with the driver; the rest of us, in back. He headed toward the center of the capital, but when we reached the intersection of Place L'Ouverture and Champs de Mars, I was stunned. Nothing I had read, no photographs I'd seen in the newspapers, could prepare me for the desperation of the occupants of countless ragged tents lining the median strip of the broad boulevard. More tarp structures sprawled on the once-green lawns of the National Palace. It was bare and brown, and smelled of human waste.

On the south wing of the palace, a Haitian flag hung from a cupola. The crowds, carrying their bedding on their backs, were pressed against each other, waiting for tomorrow's presidential inauguration. Henri was their only hope. A group of seats at the front was cordoned off for dignitaries; workmen were draping a balcony with blue and red fabric, Haiti's colors.

Our driver, a Haitian Army officer, deftly maneuvered our vehicle away from the congestion, dropped the Haitian ambassador at his home, then us at Villa Teresa.

"That man sure can drive," I said. "Something about him looks so familiar."

I knocked on the glass separating the three of us from the front of the limo. Lance slid it open, and the driver turned for an instant.

"Sergeant Duval? Is it you?"

"Wi, Mis Gloria. I shaved off my moustache and goatee, but I've been waiting for you to recognize me. I've been promoted to captain. See the silver bars on my epaulets? I didn't want to appear too pushy."

"How could I forget you? You found me blackboards and chalk, paper and crayons, when no one else helped us. I couldn't have kept the school going without you."

"*Tout au tande,* all of you listen. She cared for our neglected children with amore and took nothing for herself. My men and I scrounged through dilapidated school buildings and paper factories looking for supplies. We would get her anything she needed, even if we had to steal it."

You could hear a pin drop in the limo.

"The children wept when she left. Welcome back, Mis Gloria."

Lance seemed impressed. "Why didn't you tell me more about the school?"

"You were always so busy that we didn't have time to talk. How did my young ones do, Captain Duval?"

"Pretty good. You trained the volunteer college students well."

"And Mr. Green?"

"I call him Mickey now. We sometimes have a beer together after I make a delivery. He and his men are still building houses near the Copa Otel, and there's a long waiting list for them."

"The casino?"

"Up and running. We look the other way because it's bringing in money for lumber, nails, and other building materials."

The architecture of the villa showed a French influence. They'd ruled the island until the slaves revolted in the nineteenth century. The rich continued to furnish their homes in Parisian fashion, and the natives copied them on a smaller scale. They also continued keeping slaves—*restaveks,* or "stay-withs," as they are called.

A table had been set in the garden, and a maid who couldn't have been more than fourteen years old served lunch.

The first course was cold squash soup.

"This is a side of Haiti I didn't know existed, Lance."

"At the expense of the poor," Uberto muttered.

"Most people don't," Lance said. "Even before the quake, ordinary people were lucky to have rice, beans, and bananas for supper."

"That'll change," Uberto yelled. "After tomorrow, it'll all be different."

"It's not Lance and Gloria's fault, darling." Donna tried to placate her husband. "Education, that's what this country needs. Free education."

I tugged at the arm of the young server.

"Do you go to school, dear?" I asked, as she put a sweet potato roll at each of our places.

"Sometimes, madam."

"It's not polite to ask so many questions, Gloria, The young women are embarrassed enough," Lance whispered to me.

The entree was grilled goat cubes marinated in orange and lemon juice, accompanied by brown rice. It was delicious.

"The Haitian Embassy sent tickets for the folk ballet tonight. It'll be performed at the ballroom of the Hotel Oloffa; no theatres were left standing after the quake. It starts at seven, and it would be impolite not to attend. So let's unpack. The next few days will be active ones."

"You're right, Lance," Donna added. "Come Uberto, you need to relax."

Lance and I had a beautiful room in the east wing of the inn. It had a canopied bed with sheer curtains on its sides. The linen smelled of lilacs. I stood in front of him and unbuttoned the bodice of my sleeveless dress. Lance slipped it over my head, and then unhooked my bra. With one hand, he fondled my breasts, and with the other unzipped his trousers and let them fall to the ground. As he stepped out of them, I thought I heard him sigh, "I love you, Gloria."

We took off the rest of our clothes and he led me into the bathroom.

The private bathtub was large enough for two. He helped me step over the high side into the tub, and then got in beside me. I soaped him first; then it was Lance's turn. He fondled my breasts, my belly, and the inside of my thighs as he lathered my body. Using the hand-held showerhead, we rinsed off together, towel dried one another, and headed for the comfort of the bed.

It was only afternoon. There would be plenty of time to unpack and dress for the evening.

The following morning, Captain Duval arrived at Villa Teresa at nine a.m. We had just finished breakfast and were ready to leave for the National Palace.

"Ana," I called to the young serving girl, "Do you have any small bottles of iced water we can take with us in a cooler?"

She seemed confused. Lance interceded and asked her the same question in a mixture of French and Creole.

"Wi," she said, smiled at me, and went into the kitchen.

"Gloria, do you have a hat? The inauguration ceremony and speeches could take hours. It's ninety degrees already."

"Oh, I forgot. I'll go back to our room to get it."

"Hurry, the captain is impatient."

I returned in seconds wearing a broad-brimmed, blue straw hat that matched my sundress and I carried a tube of sunscreen in my hand. Lance and the agriculturists were already in the limo, as was a cooler with water and some paper cups. I was anxious to see Henri one more time, if only from a distance. Would my heart pound again as it once had, or would I accept the inevitable change in the pattern of our lives?

Captain Duval got out of the driver's seat, opened the back door, and helped me in with a broad smile and a pleasing, *"bon maten."*

No one seemed to know exactly when the inauguration ceremonies would begin, but Lance thought we should get there early before the crowds became impassable.

Captain Duval was dressed in a plain beige suit.

"No uniform, today, captain?"

"I don't want to be *konsomasyon*—conspicuous. Is that the right word, Mis Gloria?"

"Wi, but I can see the outline of your gun against your jacket. Push it further into your pants."

"Mesi," he said, and we both laughed as he readjusted his firearm.

❧

The captain drove the limo to a field behind the National Palace that was reserved for dignitaries' cars. From there we walked around the building to the south wing. The beating of steel drums resounded through the area.

"No Woman, No Cry," a top-ten Haitian song, blasted from a public address system that had been installed for the occasion. Some of those waiting to see Henri Betencourt were dancing;

others were sitting on the ground, peeling mangoes and eating oranges. Mothers, breasts exposed, were nursing their babies.

Signs were everywhere. "Hurrah Henri." "Where Is Eldridge Bayou? Why Was he Bumped Off the Ballot?" "We Need Jobs." "The Betencourts Win Again." "Down With the Electoral Council." "We Want Eldridge, We Want Democracy." "My Family Is Still Hungry." Henri's victory hadn't unified the people.

There were angry faces in the crowd. The chanting grew louder. It was scary.

"There is the *blan madanm,*" someone yelled, blocking our path. The voice was familiar; the face was not.

Trouble was brewing. Captain Duval, his hand on his pistol, pushed him aside. We followed close behind. Lance grasped my hand. I couldn't stop trembling, and, feeling it, he tightened his grip. When we reached the cordoned-off section, the senator showed the military guards our special tickets and we were seated.

Muttering under his breath, a small, ragged man, unshaved and dirty, stood outside the roped-off area biting on the stub of a cigarette. He carried a piece of irregular cardboard with some writing scribbled on it.

"What does it say? I asked Lance.

"Strange. It reads, "You killed my daughter and her baby. Henri Betencourt, you aren't fit to be president of Haiti."

My mind replayed earlier events in my relationship with Henri…dinner at his uncle's house…Lucia stalking me…her pregnancy, her rape and consequent murder…and in between those ugly memories, the best lovemaking I'd ever had. I had completely been his woman, and nothing else mattered. How was it that someone I'd loved without reservation had done such ugly things and made so many enemies?

The cheers and slogans continued around us. So did the music.

Suddenly, the music stopped. Everyone grew quiet except the children. A young male vocalist stepped out on the balcony, and the crowd roared its approval. I had no idea who he was, but when the handsome tenor began singing the Haitian national anthem, everyone stood and saluted the flag.

(Creole)

♪ *Pou Ayati zanset yo*
Se pou n mache men nan lamen
Nan mitan n pa fet pou gen tret
Nou fet pou n sel met tet nou
Annou mache men nan lamen
Pou Ayiti ka vin pi bel
Annou met, et tet amsam
Pou Ayiti onon tout zanset yo.
Annou, annow met tet ansanm ♪

(English)

♪ *For our country,*
For our forefathers,
United let us march.
Let there be no traitors in our ranks!
Let us be masters of our soil.
United let us march
For our country,
For our forefathers. ♪

Thousands of voices joined the singer. The anthem had five stanzas, and everyone seemed to know the words. Women screamed in ecstasy and pulled at their dreadlocks; men beat their chests. The old and the young wept.

The newly appointed archbishop of Haiti entered the balcony wearing a white miter with green crosses, and a green robe. A gold rosary on a chain of yellow amber beads hung around his neck, and he carried a large gold cross. Pierre Betencourt and several judges in black robes followed him onto the balcony.

The archbishop raised his arms; the crowd bowed their heads and listened.

"Haiti is the broken body of Jesus," he began, and continued by encouraging the Haitians to unite under the new president and rebuild the country with sacrifice and faith in God.

The sound of the steel drums grew louder. Handsome as ever, Henri Betencourt stepped out on the balcony, and the others parted so he could stand before the archbishop. Pierre handed the prelate a family bible. Henri placed his hand on it.

For an instant, I felt such pride. But I could never have been his first lady. In those few months, we had loved each other with total abandonment, but the transition to life outside the bedroom would have been impossible.

So here I was, sitting beside Lance Carter. He was intelligent, generous, kind, and passionate, and he seemed to love me. I began to see the possibility of happiness in my future.

"I swear," Henri said, "for the love of my country and the love of my God to work ceaselessly to rebuild my country from the destruction brought upon it by the recent earthquake, even if I die doing it. I am first of all a Haitian, then a man, and a citizen of the world. Unite and work with me. I shall not disappoint you."

The archbishop uttered a few words in Latin that I did not understand. The spectators stopped chewing on their peanuts and shouted "amen." A gunshot rang out, shattering the solemn mood of the crowd.

The newly elected president fell to the ground.

Everyone started running out of the grounds or towards the dais. Men were swinging machetes randomly as they pushed and shoved each other. The glint of their weapons made me shiver. Chaos erupted. Sirens resonated across the field. Men in army uniforms appeared from every corner, separated the crowds with the butts of their rifles, and made room for an ambulance rushing to reach the National Palace.

None of us knew whether Henri was dead or alive, not even the ragged man who may have been Lucia's father. He did not try to run away, but stood glued to his spot with his old, smoking pistol raised in the air.

Two uniformed officers approached and took him away.

❧ Chapter Twenty ❧

I sprang out of my seat, raising the rope separating the shooter and me. I tried to duck under it and run toward the balcony, but tripped on a stone. There was screaming all around us; war cries and words of hate were coming from every group. The limited number of military officers could not control the melee.

A gang of young men, each wearing red bandanas, was punching out a gang sporting green bandanas. The reds were followers of Henri Betencourt; the greens had favored his opponent and were glad that someone had tried to assassinate the new president. Machetes and switchblades were swinging, and wounds were inflicted on both sides. Blood began to flow, and soon the dry, brown ground was red.

Women grabbed their children and ran as far away from the violence as their legs would carry them. Police sirens filled the air, and Army units reinforced the soldiers already on the scene.

All I wanted was to reach Henri, to hold him, to comfort him. One of the lecherous gang members lunged toward me. Lance's long arms reached out, and he dragged me, by my legs, back under the ropes into the safety of the cordoned off area.

I was an earth-stained mess.

"No," he commanded, "you cannot go to Henri now. It's unsafe for a white woman to be alone. Wait, I'll get you there. I

194

know about you and Henri, but I don't care. I loved you from the first time we met in Jacmel."

"Why should you love me? Why should anyone love me?"

"Many reasons, my Gloria."

I was too frantic to process Lance's words. All I could think about was the old man's sign, but maybe I should have paid more attention to his disjointed words when I first heard them.

"I thought I heard the old man call out, 'You rich bastard! It's because of you that Lucia and her baby are dead. It was a boy.' I didn't see a gun. I thought it was the ranting of a crazy old man and didn't imagine that Henri was in mortal danger. I should have told Captain Duval. He might have stopped him."

"That's wishful thinking, Gloria, not fact."

"Henri wanted a family, a Haitian family to replace the one he lost. I was too old to give him a child. But the groupies who hung around his political camp were young and fertile. Lucia got pregnant quickly, but he didn't love her, and he wasn't going to marry her. We were soul mates from the moment he came to my class to improve his English."

Lance shifted my body, still in his arms, and looked into my eyes. "It doesn't mean you can't love again. I loved my wife for thirty-five years, but she's gone. My sons are grown men with families of their own. I think I told you that we adopted them in Port-au-Prince when they were young boys."

"Yes, you did."

"There will always be a connection to Haiti for you and me. We deserve a second chance at love. Man was not meant to be alone until eternity."

He drew me closer to his chest. I could hear his heart beating. His affectionate preaching calmed my trembling body and lifted my soul from despair.

The crowd thinned out as the ambulance left for the hospital. Rumors could be heard amongst the small remaining groups.

"The shooter was the father of Betencourt's 'ho'."

"I heard she was pregnant."

"Yeah, but she was raped anyway by a gang of hoods."

"She died in premature childbirth at the tent hospital run by the white women."

"The baby was stillborn."

I wanted to scream out, "You bastards, we did everything possible to save her and the child."

Lance covered my mouth gently.

"This is not the time to anger these wild men."

Captain Duval escorted Donna and Uberto to a public cab and gave the driver instructions to return them to the Villa Teresa.

When most of the crowd had dispersed, carrying their discontent to the streets, Lance and I walked across the grounds to the building below the balcony. We could see Pierre Betencourt picking up Henri's personal belongings. He held a Rolex I recognized in one hand, and the bloodied family bible in the other.

No one knew whether Henri was dead or alive. The priests had gone in the ambulance with him.

"Pierre!" Lance called up to the balcony. "Come downstairs, we'll drive you to the hospital."

Pierre leaned over the balcony. "Gloria, is that you?"

I nodded.

"Are you with Senator Carter?"

"Yes."

Lance gave me a quizzical look that seemed to say "the brother, too?" It was not, however, the time to explain my friendship with Pierre.

"I'll be right there," Pierre called down. "If Henri is still alive, we may need your help, Senator Carter."

By that time there was enough room for Captain Duval to drive the limo onto the grounds of the National Palace. Lance, Pierre, and I got into the back and we sped off to St. Clare's Hospital.

I gave Pierre a consoling hug and let a few tears run down my face. Lance gave me that odd look again, and then telephoned the American embassy.

"The new president of Haiti has been shot. He's probably in St. Clare's Hospital by now. We don't know if he's dead, alive, or badly wounded. Thanks. I'll depend on you to alert all available surgeons to be on call if needed. Is the medical equipped airplane on the ground should we need to fly him to the United States?"

Still holding the phone, Lance turned to Pierre. "Do you know Henri's blood type?"

"We're brothers, so I hope it's the same as mine—AB."

A dozen Haitian soldiers stood guard outside the hospital. Crudely tied bouquets of flowers had been placed at the gate surrounding the medical compound. Holding their crucifixes in their wrinkled hands, old women were praying on their knees for the president's recovery. News traveled fast.

The three of us walked up a long flight of steps to the entrance. Pierre spoke to the captain and showed him his credentials. They smiled at each other and shook hands. Pierre walked through the security checkpoint and waited for us inside the hospital.

Then it was Lance's and my turn. They patted us down and searched my bag, then allowed us into the hospital foyer where we joined Dr. Betencourt. Solemn but hopeful, we approached the waiting room reserved for the relatives of those still in surgery.

Henri's brother spoke to an elderly nurse who was sitting at the front desk. She wore a stiff white cap, a vestige of the years when French nuns ran the hospital.

"Good afternoon. I'm President Betencourt's brother, Pierre. Is it possible to have this conversation in English so Senator Lance and Mis Gloria can understand what we are saying?"

"I know who you are, Dr. Betencourt. I remember when you were a promising young intern at this hospital, but you left us for America. Who are the two with you?"

"The senator is an ally, a representative of the US government; the woman is more than a close friend of our president. How is my brother doing?"

"Sorry, there's nothing I can tell you. President Betencourt is still in surgery. They are doing everything they can to save him. Please, have a seat. His doctor will be out shortly."

It sounded ominous. There was not a bit of optimism in her voice. The waiting room was a sad place. An old lady was praying, lips moving, hands cupped towards heaven. A little girl cuddled in her mother's arms was crying, "I want my daddy."

Everyone was waiting for a doctor to appear and say that his or her loved one would be all right. Most of the patients had been knifed or beaten up at the melee following the inauguration.

I clung to Lance as we sat down on a worn gray sofa. The warmth of his body neutralized the chills that were running through mine. I was scared, but it didn't keep me from praying that Henri would recover, assume the presidency, and give me one more opportunity to hold him for a moment before we said our final orevwa. Although I'd always love this country, my future was in the United States with Lance Carter.

Lance observed the scene somberly, his serious face lit by his piercing blue eyes. With one hand, he texted the events of the day to his staff, and with the other he soothed the tension in my neck and shoulders.

How many men can a woman cry for? My husband had died long after he'd stopped being my lover and was finally buried. He lived at home until his mind faded into nothingness, and he no longer recognized even me when I visited him at the lockdown facility.

Mickey longed for the freedom to regain his youth, if only for a moment. So did I, but when I found out he belonged to another woman—who, incidentally, loved him—I wouldn't break up their marriage. Henri was the unselfish lover women dreamed of, passionate and possessive, yet controlled and able to satisfy a lustful female partner.

Lance would never be like any of them, but he loved me with a depth of feeling that made me happy and safe and eager to love him back. I might have to share him with the President of the United States; that was a small sacrifice. At this age, it was good to feel secure in a man's arms.

The door from the operating theater opened into the waiting room. A doctor with a well-trimmed mustache and tortoise-rimmed glasses came in, looked around, and headed to Pierre, who was sitting opposite us in a club chair as gray and worn as the sofa.

Pierre rose. The surgeon put his hand on his shoulder.

"I'm sorry, Dr. Betencourt. We did everything we could. The bullet was too close to your brother's heart. Henri is dead."

Pierre looked at us, but did not speak. His expression told us everything. We stepped to his side. I took his hand.

"May I see him, Pierre?"

"I think not. The vice presidential candidate is on his way here. So is Archbishop Jacques Totu, who will swear him in as the president pro tem until the next election."

"And then can I see him?" Gloria asked.

"Sorry, only relatives are allowed in to see the dead."

Tears flowed down my face. Alive or dead, I'd hoped to see Henri once more.

"After the president pro tem and the archbishop leave, I want to spend the night here with my brother. Alone. Tomorrow," he continued, "there will be a state funeral instead of a celebration."

"We understand," Lance said. "I'll contact the state department and ask permission to represent our country at the funeral."

"That is kind of you. Now take Gloria to the hotel, Senator Carter. She's a very special woman. She taught my brother how to love again when his world was crushed and he'd fled to Florida to escape the reality of his family's murder. Treat her well. It is not good to grow old alone."

"Are you sure you don't want us to stay with you longer?"

"No, go now. We will meet again. Maybe even here in Haiti, when the world grows saner and my country is beautiful once more."

❧ *Epilogue* ❧

I sold the apartment in Florida and moved into Lance's suite at the Mayflower Hotel in Washington, DC. Life was good. We planned a June wedding surrounded by our immediate families.

Lance continued trying to improve the lot of the million Haitians who were still homeless. He helped their government sort out land claims so large tracts of houses could finally be built. I raised money, collected clothes, and recruited volunteers by lecturing at the many women's clubs in the capital.

I hadn't heard a word from Dr. Betencourt or Mickey, and that was as it should be. The DC newspapers carried pictures of Dr. Joseph Abudu, a renowned philosophy professor, who had been Henri Betencourt's running mate. Dr Abudu was sworn in as president pro tempore at Henri's deathbed to preserve the stability of the country.

A few weeks before Lance's and my wedding, a package from Port-au-Prince arrived for me. It contained a handcrafted silver necklace and a note from Pierre Betencourt.

Dear Gloria:

Henri was in the process of having this silver and enamel necklace made for you by a famous local jeweler. I made sure it was finished. The enameled panels in red and blue represent Haiti's blood and strength, the palm tree her beauty, and the cannons her courage.

Wear it and remember that he loved you.

Here's wishing you happiness in future years with Lance Carter. He's a good man.

Fondly,

Pierre Betencourt, MD

Haitian/English Translation Key

Words and Phrases (in alphabetical order)

Haitian	**English**
Ak	and
Alo	hello
amore amoure, amourez	love, lover
Ankouraje	encourage
antre zanmi mwen	meantime, my friend
aplodi	bravo
atansyon	attention
bat, bravo	applaud, cheer
biskwit	biscuit, biscuits
blan madanm	white woman
bon chans	good luck
bon jou	good day
bon maten	good morning
bon nwit	good night
bon zanmi	good friends
bonswa	goodnight, good evening
chokola	chocolate
dis minit	ten minutes
enfimye	nurse
entranjes	foreigners
famasi	pharmacy

famasyent	pharmacist
fanm	woman, women
foutbol	soccer
foutbole	soccer player
fri-bannanns	fried bananas
gaga	idiot
grenadye	pomegranate-like fruit
kafi	coffee
kola	cola
konsomasyon	conspicuous
la fanmi	the family
lakay, kay	home, dwelling
lakay peson	nobody home
mal damou	love sickness
manbo	voodoo priestess
mesi	thanks
mis	miss
moun	male
moun gason	male persons
msye	mister; mr.
mwen	my
mwen adore ou dous mwen	I adore you my sweet
mwen renmen ou	I love you
mwen vajen	my vagina
nouvo komansman	new beginnings

nouvo pati politik ....new party political

oke li te genyen ....well, he has won

orevwa .... goodbye

otel..hotel

ou mesi .... thank you

ovai.. future

pen ak konfitti .... bread and strawberry jam

pouding dire .... rice pudding

prezidan .... president

restaveks ....slaves, "stay-withs"

sikre te .... sweet tea

tant..aunt

te..tea

tonton.. uncle

tout au tande................................. all of you listen

wi.. yes

yo nan mitan janm mwen .. the lips between my legs

zanmi ....friends

❧ About Janet S. Kleinman ❧

Janet Kleinman makes her home in South County, Florida. She is a member of a Writers Study Group and Education VP of her local chapter of an international philanthropic organization. A cum laude graduate of Brooklyn College, she holds a master's degree from Manhattan College in New York City. The author has written collateral materials for Fortune 500 companies and also taught English to middle school students and recent immigrants. Her articles have appeared in such publications as Writer's Digest, The South Florida Times, and Lifestyles. *Flirting with Disaster* is her first published novel.